By: Rebecca Gober & Courtney Nuckels

Clean Teen Publishing

SURVIVING ELE

CLEAN TEEN
PUBLISHING

Cover Design by: Marya Heiman
Typography by: Courtney Nuckels
Editing by: Cynthia Shepp

Content Disclosure

For more information about our content disclosure, please utilize the QR code above with your smart phone or visit us at

www.cleanteenpublishing.com.

I heed not that my earthly lot
Hath little of Earth in it—
That years of love have been forgot
In the hatred of a minute:--
I mourn not that the desolate
Are happier, sweet, than I,
But that you sorrow for my fate
Who am a passer-by.

- "To---" by: Edgar Allan Poe

ONE

I can see the thinning tree line peek above the horizon. The safe house is near. I question whether I'll have enough time to get there and save everyone before he catches up with me. My heart is pounding like a drum in my chest. Every breath I take feels like sharp spikes stabbing through my lungs. I push my powers to the extreme, using every last seed of energy to beat him.

"Slow down, sugar. You don't want to bring all of those innocent people into this, do you?" Zack's voice penetrates my thoughts.

I've been listening to his rants for the last two miles. I don't know how far this ability reaches. Is he a mile behind me or a few yards? I don't dare turn around and refuse to answer him. I miss dodging a low-lying branch and it scrapes viciously against my cheek. Wiping at my stinging face, I do my best not to slow down when my hand comes back streaked with red. With no energy to try to heal myself and keep my speed up, I leave it be.

"Are you going to put your dad in danger because of this? Just give yourself up! What about that cute little brother of yours? I think you call him Sabby," he taunts me.

1

I nearly stop dead in my tracks at the sound of my sweet brother's name coming from that horrible monstrosity of a man. *"Don't you ever speak his name. I will kill you, Zack! If you don't turn around now, you'll have forced my hand and I will take you out just like I took out your father."* An angry red haze begins clouding my vision.

Zack seems unaffected by the mention of my killing his father. *"I think you forget who it is that chases you right now. If you wish to take him out..."* he pauses to make sure the word *him* sinks in nice and deep, *"...then be my guest."*

An icy chill runs up my spine and mixes with the heat that my body is pouring out. I find myself gasping for breath as I continue to push myself towards the safe house. Hearing Zack's voice made it easy to forget the person who is really chasing me. *Tony.* I clutch my hand to my chest as if I can keep my heart from spilling open onto the forest floor.

Zack laughs hideously inside my thoughts. *"You did forget..."*

I shut it off in that moment and break the line of communication that I thought was meant for only Tony and me to share. I don't have to listen to any of it!

I push myself harder as I break through the tree line. The safe house is only a matter of yards away now. I need to get everyone's attention. "Help!" I yell as loudly as I can. It's hard to grasp the breath needed to call to them. "Hel...!" I end the last part of the word in a coughing fit.

The doors to the hotel slam open and people start spilling out to help me. I hunch over, placing my hands on my knees, and gasp for breath.

"Willow!" Alec, my ex-boyfriend, comes bounding towards me first. His face is masked with concern. He rushes to my aid and pulls me into his arms, giving me some much-needed comfort.

I lean my head against his chest; my breath comes out in huge, jagged inhales and exhales. My heart has gone up into my ears and I can feel the blood coursing into my head, making me dizzy. Now I know why you're supposed to walk it off after a run like that. Within a few seconds, I begin to feel better again. I know it's because Alec used his healing ability on me.

Not needing him to keep me stable any longer, I take a slight step back from Alec and look around. A crowd of people surrounds us now. "We have to get out of here. They're coming," I say as loudly as I can, so everyone can hear.

"What do you mean? Who's coming?" Alec asks me. An uneasy panic fills his face as he tries to understand what I'm saying.

"Zack and his army," I say with certainty. I suppress my desire to give in and rest. Too much is on the line now; I can't let anything happen to these people.

Alec's eyes widen. Everyone thought that Zack had died when I caused an entire building to come tumbling down on top of him two days ago. Alec opens his mouth to question me but stops when we hear someone yelling.

"Willow!" My heart lurches in my chest at the sound of his real voice calling for me from across the clearing. We all turn our heads in unison to see Tony standing at the edge of the trees. His arms are crossed over his chest and his expression is calculating. He's too far away for anyone to truly see the red in his eyes.

"Is Tony hurt too?" Alec asks from behind me.

I don't know how to answer that. Yes, he's hurt. He's no longer himself. An evil monster is controlling the man I've fallen for.

"Tony?" I hear Claire call out nearby, from within the crowd. She begins to wade through the people to get to Tony and make sure he's okay. I see her pale blonde hair and petite form come to the front of the group, only a few feet from Alec and me.

"Stop!" I yell to her.

She looks bewildered as she stops and turns to look at me, her purple eyes filled with confusion.

I turn my sights on Tony again. He stands tall and unmoving, looking vigilantly near the corner of the tree line. His copper hair is disheveled by the wind. Everything within me wants to go to him, to take his hand in mine, and pretend that everything is okay. Pretend that my Tony isn't lost somewhere within his own mind.

To keep from doing so, I reach behind me and grasp onto Alec's shirt. I'm using him to tether me to this place, as an anchor, to keep me from running into the trap set forth in front of me.

"What's wrong?" Alec whispers in my ear. He steps closer; his posture is tense and alert.

I shake my head, not sure how to answer his

question. *Everything, everything is wrong.*

Tony takes a step forward. "Willow!" he yells to me again.

"Stay back, Tony!" I scream at him. Alec moves to take a step in front of me, having recognized the fear in my voice. I clench his shirt tightly to keep him in place. I hold my shaking hand out in front of me. "I mean it! Go back now or I *will* have to hurt you!" My voice trembles at the end. Will I be able to do this if I have to? Can I really hurt Tony?

He tests me by taking one more step forward.

That's not Tony! It's Zack controlling Tony. I have to repeat this mantra over and over again in my head. I hate this! The complete unfairness of the situation peaks my anger. The gold haze begins lining my vision as my outstretched hand moves an inch to the right, focused on a large evergreen that towers above him. The tree begins shaking, causing the earth underneath Tony's feet to quake. I watch him look from the tree to me with horror as he does his best to keep his balance.

"Leave now, or else!" I yell again.

At this point Mr. Leroy, who I now call Lee, and several others, have come to the front and are holding their weapons out for Tony to see. I'm amazed that Lee would trust me in such a way that he would aim his pistol at Tony. Tony is his friend; he was my mother's second in command. They've fought many a battle alongside one another.

I push the thought of my mom, who died all too recently, to the back of my mind and focus on making the earth shake some more. "Now!" I yell again to Tony, hoping he'll find me intimidating.

Even from this distance, I can see the angry glare he gives me. I've never seen such a look come from him. Well, at least not one directed at me for that matter. Goosebumps run up and down my arms and I shiver uncontrollably. Alec, noticing this, puts his arms on the back of my shoulders to support me.

Finally, Tony turns around. "Later then!" he yells before he darts back into the woods.

With my mind, I let go of the tree that I was ready to rip from the earth. I lean back into Alec, accepting his support as I exhale the breath I'd been holding for so long.

Alec holds onto me tightly from behind. I know he's worried about me. I can feel it emanating from him. I also know that he's healing me as we speak. I'm not hurt, physically at least. He doesn't really know that, so I accept the gift he's using on me.

Everyone allows me a minute to compose myself, but the questions in their eyes remain. I let go of Alec and stand upright, looking at Lee. "We have to leave this place now. Zack and his people will be coming after me. I can leave you and go out on my own to divert them, but first I need to make sure you get to safety."

Lee gives me a calm look. I'm surprised at how well he keeps his cool. Did he not just have to aim his gun at Tony, his friend? "Slow down, Willow. First, why is Zack coming after you? Or do you mean all of us?" Lee asks me.

I shake my head. "No, he wants *me*. He thinks

I'm the key to making him more powerful. He's found a way..." I think better of telling them the exact way Zack thinks I can give him powers...through my blood. The last thing I need is for any of these people to go along with the same harebrained scheme and get the stupid idea to start draining me dry.

Zack injected some of my blood into him and it somehow gave him the same gifts I have, which is way too much power for someone so evil to have. The problem for him though is that it wore off. Now he wants to keep me around to basically drip me dry so he can have an unlimited source of power.

I still don't know the full extent as to why I have so many abilities and not just one power like everyone else. All I know is that for some reason, when I'm around a person with a different power, I absorb the ability to use the same power shortly after coming in contact with them. I am the only one we know about that can do this, other than Reapers. It's sick that they have the ability to be so cold and heartless. I guess they aren't really human in the true sense. We believe the shot they gave themselves that was supposed to kill them, actually killed off the portion of their brain that causes them to have emotions and to care about others.

I think that the small amount of the Reaper shot I accidentally took at the beginning of this whole ordeal is what has given me these gifts. After all, in a way, I *am* part Reaper. But, it is a speculation that I can't prove. Unlike those monsters though, *I* am in touch with my humanity, so I don't take everything when I acquire a new gift. In fact, I don't even realize I am taking anything until one day I find myself able to do the same things they can do.

In his search for power, Zack went so far as to cause me to run into more people with different gifts because when he injects himself with my blood, he only gets the powers I had at the time the blood was taken. To top everything off, now this sicko has found a way to turn my boyfriend against me. He injected him with something that I thought was a Reaper shot. Instead, it was a new shot that I don't know much about yet. All I know is that it makes Tony a puppet that Zack can control. I don't know the extent of the control or how to reverse the effects. All I know is that my healing abilities couldn't stop the onset of the change within Tony. It only delayed it.

A thought pops into my mind. I wonder how many other people were injected with that shot Tony was given. Could some of the people we recently saved be in jeopardy of turning? If I can even get these people to safety, will they ever truly be safe?

Lee clears his throat and I realize I've gone silent in thought for a while. I decide to give him a condensed version of what's going on. "I'm sorry," I tell him. "Well, obviously as you can tell from what I've already shared, Zack is still alive."

Lee nods his head. "Yeah, I got that much already but what does Zack have to do with Tony?"

"He injected Tony with something that has turned him into someone different...someone that Zack controls.

He is making Tony come after me so he can take me to wherever Zack is hiding. You all are not safe with me around, but you aren't safe here either. To put it bluntly, you need to leave. Also, I don't know how many others have been injected. Some of the people we saved could very well turn. So you have to be careful. If you see their eyes turning red, you need to get away from them...or lock them up." I didn't want to say, 'take them out.' How can that be fair? To kill someone that had no choice of becoming what they will become. "I'll need to take some supplies and food with me, but then I'll get out of here so you all can stay safe."

Lee holds out his hand. "Whoa. Slow down there, partner." I raise my eyebrow at him. He continues. "We'll move on to the next safe house. But you aren't separating from us. I don't give a crap if Zack or Tony is after you. You aren't going off on your own."

I shake my head.

"She won't be on her own. We'll go with her." Alec stands by my side. Connor and Claire step forward and nod their heads.

I look at them like they're crazy. "Absolutely not; you aren't going anywhere with me. It's too dangerous."

"You don't have a choice." Alec's expression turns angry. Alec can be pretty stubborn. When he has his mind made up about something, there's no changing it. "You will not just go off into the night again all alone. If you think you can do that, then we'll go after Zack on our own."

My mouth drops open as I stare at him. Alec isn't usually one to be forceful, or is it more so that he hasn't had to be forceful in the past? Would he dare do what he's threatening? My face turns red as my cheeks heat with frustration. He must not understand just how completely dangerous his plan is. I am being hunted and if something was to happen to one of them during my watch, I could never forgive myself.

Lee clears his throat again and Alec and I both turn towards him. "You'll stay with us. We together..." he gestures his hand towards the large group of able-bodied fighters ready to defend us, "...we will protect you."

I shake my head. "No, my dad and my brother are here. I want them to be safe." I don't see them anywhere in the crowd.

"This isn't up for discussion, Willow," Lee says.

My mind starts working to process everything. The most important thing for me right now is that the remaining members of my family are safe. I want my friends to be safe too, but if they will not allow me to protect them, then I can't control that. I *can* control what happens to my dad and brother though.

I match Lee's stern stare, not willing to give in. "If you will not let me go alone then I will take a group with me. You take the original people with you. I will take some of the people we saved with me. If any other fighters want to join us, they may." I can tell that Lee doesn't like my plan but I can also tell that he understands my reasoning behind the request.

When it boils down to it, Lee is a loyalist. If he can keep the kids and his original group safe, that's all that matters. He knows that I want to keep an eye on the people we recently saved because those are the only ones at risk of turning. It didn't take long for Tony to be completely taken over by Zack, so if any of these people were injected with the same shot, they could turn within a few days. I want them to be as far from my family as possible if that happens. Lee turns and looks at his people behind him, then looks back to me. "Okay. We better start preparing so we can clear out of here by dawn." He looks tired but determined.

I nod my head. "Thank you, Lee."

It's funny because the expression he gives me next is different from his usual ornery look. Instead, there is a mix of fatherly care and worry. "We'll look into a way to help stop Zack too. In the meantime, you stay safe."

I can't help but smile. Somehow, I've made a chink in his grumpy old man armor. "I will."

With that, we turn and head into the hotel. Once we've all gathered inside, I turn and face Alec, who has been on my heels this whole time. With one hand on my hip and the other one pointing angrily at him, I address him. "How dare you try to threaten to go after Zack alone? That wasn't fair!"

He looks at me like what I said was the most ridiculous statement in the universe. Instead of saying anything, he grabs the crook of my elbow and pulls me into a dark, seemingly empty conference room. He slams the door and flips on the switch of a battery-operated lantern. It casts an intimate glow throughout the small room. Alec slams the lantern down on a table and then directs his attention to me.

I'm taken aback by his actions. I've seen Alec angry before, but it still seems like such a flip from his usual relaxed persona. It's unnerving to have his anger directed at me. I find myself moving away from him until my back is up against a wall.

With nowhere left for me to go, he steps forward, closing the gap between us. "How dare *you* say you are going to go after him alone? What is your problem, Willow?"

My breath catches in my throat. Looking into his eyes, I see a mixture of emotions. Without trying, my gift of empathy takes over and suddenly all of his feelings are rolling off him in waves that I can feel, touch, and taste. I know my eyes must be pitch black as I feel everything he feels. Anger, pain, hurt, jealousy, insecurity, longing, desire... The hardest one for me to swallow is the love that he still feels for me. His emotional tornado hits me hard in the chest.

I force myself to look away. *Turn it off, Willow!* It's not right to invade his privacy with my gifts. When the emotions finally stop coming at me in overwhelming waves, I look back up at him. His expression has slightly softened.

Finding my voice, I try to reason with him. "This isn't your problem, Alec. I didn't want to drag you or anyone else into this mess with me. Zack doesn't want you. You all would be safe right now if it wasn't for me."

He puts his hand on my shoulder. The small

amount of space between us has me catching my breath again. "No. This isn't only your problem, Willow. You did nothing to deserve this. You are a victim, just like everyone else who has been hurt by those monsters! None of us will be safe until Zack is stopped." His eyes wander down to my lips for a slight second before he looks back up into my eyes. His eyes have a fire in them that was missing a second before. He lets his hand drop. I watch him press it into a fist. "What I still don't understand is how you can so easily close us out of your life. You know how I feel about you. How your friends feel about you. Yet, you run away with Tony in the middle of the night. Without even telling us where you went or if you were safe. Now you want to run away again on your own. Do you honestly think we are too weak to be included in your plans? Just because you have all of these powers doesn't mean you can take on the world alone."

I throw my hands up in frustration. "I didn't know what to do, Alec! I still don't know what to do. How am I supposed to make these decisions? I don't think you are weak at all. Can't you see that I care too much about you all to throw you in the line of danger?" My chest is tight as I let the feelings and insecurities that I've been holding onto loose. Tears start blurring my vision. "Did you know that sometimes I don't think I will make it through this? I may have all of these powers but they haven't been able to help me when I really needed it. They didn't help me save my mom. I couldn't save Tony, even though I tried." The tears start falling as I think of how hard I tried to heal Tony.

How badly I wanted to, as if my will alone could have saved him. How can I have all of this power but still feel so helpless? My voice is shaky. "I tried..." Alec pulls me into his arms. I allow myself to let out all of the emotions I've been bottling up inside.

"I know you tried. But you can't do this all alone, Willow." He brushes his hand over my curls and rubs my back soothingly.

I nod my head against his chest. "I know." I pull away and wipe at my eyes with the palms of my hands. "I don't want anything to happen to you guys though. I can't take it if I lose one more person that I love." It's not until I see his expression that I realize what I just admitted to him.

"You love him?" He says it as more of a statement than a question. His wounded look breaks something inside of me.

What do I say? "I think I may..." I can't look at Alec any longer. How can this be so hard? When I look at him, I feel like I've betrayed him in a way. I haven't tried to lead him on, to make him believe that we still have a shot. I honestly care for Alec but these feelings that I've been developing for Tony are more than I can contain. I can't stifle what my heart feels. "I'm so sorry, Alec," I say, looking back up.

He's looking away. His face is masked with pain.

"I don't know what to say to make any of this better, Alec. Please, tell me what to say. I just want to make things right between us."

He looks at me again with those deep, navy eyes.

"Tell me that you're just kidding, that you aren't really falling in love with someone else...someone who is not me." He barely whispers the last part.

I want to tell him what he wants to hear, but it wouldn't be right. Unable to speak, I stare into his eyes. I don't want to hurt him. He means too much to me. I swallow hard and tell him, "Maybe you should go with Lee."

He takes a deep breath and shakes his head. "No. I'm not leaving you." He places his hands on either side of my face. Our proximity is close enough that I can feel his breath on my skin. That angry heat returns to his expression. "Do you think that I would just leave you because you don't love me anymore?"

"Urgh!" I have to stifle the desire to stomp my feet on the ground. Alec removes his hands and takes a step back, obviously surprised by my outburst. "No, Alec! I don't think you are petty enough to leave me because I'm falling for someone else. I was just offering you a lifeline. An out! Why do you keep insisting on putting words in my mouth?"

He runs his hands through his dark hair. "Because I'm hurt." His honesty shocks me and silence fills the room as the truth floats heavily in the air.

I figured as much. I'm just amazed that he's in touch with his feelings enough to admit it. "I really won't think any less of you if you go with Lee."

He shakes his head.

"We can't fight about this if we're going to work

15

together. You need to know that I still love you too. I care deeply about you and I don't want this coming between us." "You love me as a friend," he clarifies. The pained look is still evident on his face.

I nod my head. "Yes. There will always be that part that loves you in another way. That will never go away. But if you will allow us to redirect those feelings to our friendship, I know we can work through all of this." I bite my lip, hoping I don't lose him. His friendship means everything to me.

He thinks about it for a moment, running his hand through his hair. "I don't doubt we can work through this." A look of determination replaces his hurt expression. "You have to promise me though, that you won't go running off on your own again."

I let out a tired laugh. "I know better than to make promises I can't keep. I will try to include you on whatever I do, but if things get too bad and I'm left with no choice, I will do whatever it takes to make sure you all are safe." I feel a sense of relief at being able to stand up for myself and to tell the truth. It's something I've struggled with in the past.

He rolls his eyes dramatically. "I guess I can't ask more from you than I would from myself."

I give him a hug, grateful that he can understand where I'm coming from. "Thank you for sticking by my side, Alec. It means a lot to me."

He kisses the top of my head. I try not to think more of it than I should. "Anything for you, Willow."

TWO

"We need to make the preparations," I tell Alec.

He nods his head. "I'll go get Connor and Claire. You get your father."

"My dad is *not* coming with us so I'll need to tell him goodbye – again. Will you all start packing up the supplies?" I ask.

"Yes, ma'am." Alec gives me a fake salute.

I roll my eyes but inside I'm secretly happy that our awkward moment has passed. Alec and I leave the room and head off in separate directions. The hallways in the hotel are brimming with activity. People walk every which way with candles or electric lanterns in their hands. Some people look nervous about the upcoming move; others are obviously used to it by their calm expressions.

I pass by a couple with neon-yellow eyes who seem to be arguing about where they are going to go tomorrow. From what I can hear, the woman wants to come with me to fight Zack. The man wants to go with Lee. When they notice me, they stop talking and try to act busy gathering supplies.

I give the woman a nod of my head as I pass by her

on my way to my dad's room. I knock softly on the door to their room, in case my little brother is sleeping.

"Come in," my dad calls to me.

I open the door and find him packing Sebastian's and his things. Sebastian is sleeping soundly on his bed, curled up under a heap of blankets. His little curls poke out from beneath the mess of covers. When my dad sees me, he drops the bag in his hand and runs to my side, pulling me into a hug. "Lee told me you were back. I looked for you but couldn't find you."

"I'm sorry, I got caught up. I found you as quickly as I could." I smile up at him.

He pulls me at arm's length and looks me over. His hair is now nearly fifty percent grey. He looks tired and weary. I can't help but wonder when we'll catch a break. If it's not a virus killing off most of the population, then it's mad men coming after you or Reapers trying to suck your powers dry. When will we be able to just be? It worries me that a sense of normalcy might be too much of a farfetched idea these days.

"I'm almost done packing." He looks down at me with worried copper eyes. "Lee said you aren't coming with us?"

"Dad..." I say in a defensive voice, making the 'a' drag out a little longer than I should.

He throws his hands up, stopping me. "No, I've learned enough lately to not argue with my daughter. She is a leader of the people now after all. I am still your dad though, so we need to discuss this." His voice takes a stern edge. Yep, there's the dad I know. "Now, I know you are going and that Sebastian needs me, but I need to know if *you* need me." He runs his hands through his hair as he looks from Sabby to me. "I don't know all of the reasons why you don't want us to come with you, but I can only assume that it's because of some trouble you're in. I can send Sabby with the teachers. I've thought this through a million times in my head. They can take care of him and I can come with you." His love floods over me like a veil. I can feel that love, the kind that can only come from a parent, filling me to the brim.

I shake my head. "No, Dad. He needs you right now." I point to my little brother. "Yes, there is trouble... but, I have my friends and some very strong soldiers who will be going with me. We'll be fine. There's no reason to worry."

He laughs but the apprehension doesn't fade from his expression. "Even if you were tucked safely away to where nothing could hurt you, I would still worry. That's what fathers do, we worry about our kids. It's like a full-time job all on its own." He glances over at my brother and then looks back to me. "I know that you're a very strong woman, Willow, and that you can take care of yourself. But, before you leave, I need to tell you something." He lowers his voice to more of a whisper. "I had a vision."

I try to force the tears from filling my eyes as I nod my head. "I know, Dad. I read Mom's letter."

"Your father watched you die in that vision." I remember the words in my mom's final message to me

and my heart still pangs with grief over it. My dad had a vision that I was going to be killed. Both my mom and he knew that one of them would have to lay down their life to save mine. They each wrote me a letter in the event that they succeeded in saving me. My mom's letter is the one I received. Absentmindly, I reach my hand down to where her letter sits in my pocket.

My father's face crumples at the mention of his wife. He looks down at his hands for a moment, then back up at me, regaining his composure. "We both love you so very much. Most days I wish that it was my letter you read. I would have gladly given my life for you...for her."

His eyes are wet with tears and I find myself unable to hold mine back any longer. "Oh Dad..." I cry as I pull him into a hug. We both cry quietly and, for a moment in time, we allow ourselves to mourn. Ever since my mom died, I never felt I've been able to grieve. Like there's just not time. I feel guilty every time I think about it because I know she deserves the remembrance.

My dad pats my back and when he looks back at me, the tears in his eyes have dried. "I had another vision though. Just last night."

I wipe my tears and try to compose myself. "What was it about?"

"You and Tony. He was chasing you and you were scared." My dad looks frightened as he continues. "His eyes were red."

I gently nod my head, pursing my lips.

His eyes widen. "You know?" he asks.

"Yes, but he's not a Reaper though," I clarify, wanting to make that point very clear. "I don't know what he is, but it's different. He's somehow being controlled by Zack Hastings." His name makes my stomach churn.

"Zack?" My dad asks a little too loudly. We both turn to see Sebastian stirring.

"Yes," I whisper, but soon realize we've woken up my little brother anyway.

He sits up in bed, rubbing his sleepy little eyes. "Wello?"

"Hey, Sabby." I smile and move to his side of the bed.

"You back!" He smiles and throws his small arms around me like a monkey.

I hug him tightly. "Yes, but I'm afraid I have to leave again."

He shakes his head, making his curls dance. "No, Wello. You stay here with me." He says it as if it's an order rather than a request.

I try my best to give him a brave smile. "I wish I could, Sabby. I have to go on a very important mission though." His little frown and fat bottom lip breaks my heart. I add, "It's a secret mission." I raise my finger up to my lips, hoping to improve his mood.

"Like a spy?" He perks up with interest.

I shrug my shoulders. "Kind of. I have a mission for you too, Sabby."

"Weally?" His eyes widen with excitement. I squelch a laugh at his seriously cute face.

"Yes. I need you to make sure you are the bravest boy in all of your class. If your friends get scared, you can show them how brave you are and maybe they will try to be like you. Can you do that?" I ask.

He hangs on my every word. He allows what I said to sink in, and then nods his head vigorously. "Yes, Wello! I be very brave!" He holds his arm up and flexes his little muscles. My dad and I laugh. What's funny is that there is actually a definition of muscle on those tiny arms. It's weird but probably a side effect of the shot that gave him superior strength.

"Good! I knew I could count on you. I'll come back as soon as I can. It may take a while though." His eyes lose a bit of their brightness so I add, "Don't worry, Sabby. I wouldn't leave you if I didn't know how strong you were. Daddy is strong too and he'll take good care of you."

"You strong too, Wello!" He grabs my arm, rolling up my sleeve, and prompts me to show him my muscles. I humor him and flex my arms, which makes him smile.

"Thank you, Sabby. I love you." I kiss the top of his little head.

"Wuv you too, Wello!" He hugs me once more.

I stand up and give my dad a hug. "Love you, Dad."

"I love you too, honey. Please stay safe," he says in my ear so Sabby can't hear.

"I will," I tell him in a whisper. I keep thinking about the visions I've had of Tony catching up with me. I don't let on that I'm scared though. The last thing my dad needs right now is an additional worry. A thought occurs to me. "Dad, did you see what happened in your vision? With Tony chasing me. How did it end?"

With his hand on my upper arm he gently guides me towards the door, further away from Sebastian's hearing range. He looks at me uneasily. "In the end he catches you."

I take in an audible breath of air, knowing that's how my vision played out as well. "And then?" I wonder if he's seen further than I have.

"Then *your* eyes turn red," he says uncomfortably.

I instinctively reach my hand up to my eyes and touch the delicate skin below them. "My eyes? They turn red?"

He nods slowly.

I don't know what this means. Perhaps he makes me so angry that my inner Reaper comes out. Does that mean that I'll kill Tony? My stomach churns and bile rises in my throat. I force myself to put on a brave facade. "It's okay, Dad. We've made visions change before. If I've done it once, I can do it again."

He nods his head but the worry lines on his forehead don't smooth out any. "Please send for me if you need anything, honey. I will be there in a heartbeat." He pulls me into another hug.

"I will, Dad. You just keep Sabby safe. I'll be back as soon as I can. Just know that it will take time. If I can find a way to send word to you every once in a while, I will," I assure him.

He gives me a weak smile and kisses the top of my head before allowing me to leave.

After I say my goodbyes one last time, I head out to finish making preparations. Downstairs, I find everyone in the dining hall. Piles of supplies and equipment are mounded up on the tables. I find my friends at the back of the cafeteria and join in on helping them pack.

"I'm glad you're back," Connor says as he stuffs a package of marshmallows into his bag.

"Me too," I say, even though we are about to turn around and leave again in the morning.

Alec, who's loading bullets into a magazine, eyes the marshmallows and teases Connor. "Are you going to defend us with your marshmallow shooter? Is it a semi-automatic or a blow gun that you are planning to use to take out Zack?"

"Hey, marshmallows aren't just fluff!" Connor pulls the bag out and throws it hard at Alec.

It hits Alec on his shoulder. He places the last few bullets and the magazine on the table, and then playfully grabs his shoulder with his hand and acts wounded. "Ouch!" he jokes as he picks the bag up off the ground and throws it back at Connor.

Claire catches it before it hits Connor in the face. "Come on, boys." She tries to give them a stern talking to, but in the end, she can't keep the smile from her face.

I probably have the best group of friends anyone could ask for, I think to myself as I watch them. They give me an ounce of normalcy that I need in this crazy life.

After the dining hall has thinned out a bit and most of its occupants have retired to their rooms with their packed bags, Lee approaches our group. "Did you get everything you need?" he asks me.

I nod my head once. "Yes, thank you."

He looks at our bags and then back to me. "Good. I wanted to let you know that I've given our soldiers the opportunity to decide which group they'll be going with. We'll determine everyone's final choice at dawn before we leave. This will give everyone an opportunity to sleep on their decisions and say their goodbyes."

I shiver. Goodbye sounds so final, but in times like this, optimism is a luxury some of us can't afford to have. "Thank you, Lee."

He nods his head. His bright yellow eyes soften a tad. "You need to make an attempt at sleeping, Willow. You are going to need to have a clear mind in the morning."

"Thank you, I'll try." I don't foresee myself getting any sleep tonight but I humor him anyway.

"Goodnight," Lee says as he heads out of the dining hall.

"He's right, you should get some sleep. You look exhausted," Alec tells me once Lee is out of earshot.

"Thanks," I say sarcastically as I stretch my arms over my head and try not to yawn. "I better head up then."

"I'll walk you to your room," Alec offers.

I shrug my shoulders. "Okay, thanks," I say, even though it's not necessary for him to walk with me. I know he's just trying to be nice though. We both say goodnight to Connor and Claire before they head off to their separate rooms, hand in hand.

Alec's hand flinches a little as we walk towards my room. Back in the day, his hand would be occupied by mine, but not anymore. When we get to my door I reach for the knob, but Alec stops me by gently putting his hand over mine. I look up at him. I can feel the tug-o-war that is going on with his emotions.

He looks down into my eyes. "Willow, you are sixteen years old." I cock an eyebrow at him, unsure where he's going with this. He continues. "You may have some superhuman powers but you aren't superhuman. I want you to know that it's okay for you to feel scared. In fact, it wouldn't be normal if you weren't scared."

I hold my breath and my jaw tenses at his words. "I don't have time to be scared, Alec."

"It's not a matter of whether you have time or not. At the end of the day, you are still going to feel what you feel. I'm not asking you to admit to me that you're scared; all I want is for you to know that I'm here for you. I *will* protect you."

I open my mouth to speak but he raises a hand to stop me.

The candle I'm holding reflects in his navy eyes. It makes him look even more impassioned as he continues. "Don't think I'm saying this out of any ulterior motive. I will protect you, Willow Mosby, because I love you and will always love you. Before you get all freaked out let me add, I love you like a friend. I take care of my friends."

I exhale. My heart is feeling warm from his words. I'm not sure how true the 'like a friend' part of his statement is but I'll take it either way. "Thank you." The look he gives me unarms me. I look down at my feet, feeling an ounce of shame when I add, "I'm always scared, Alec."

He places a gentle finger under my chin and lifts up so I'm forced to look at him. He says, "Me too." Then he gives me a soft smile and pulls me into him, holding onto me tightly. I allow myself to feel safe in his embrace. There are no other motives behind the hug so I let the security fill that emptiness inside me. He squeezes a little tighter to let me know that it's okay. My mind contemplates both of our admissions. He's right, this is a scary world, and it's okay to admit it. The fact that we have friends to get us through it is what matters. Thanks to God, we don't have to be alone in this.

"Thank you," I say into Alec's chest.

When I step towards my door again, Alec doesn't say anything to me about the tears in my eyes. Instead, he gives me an understanding nod and then says, "Goodnight, Willow."

"Goodnight," I tell him as I open the door and go into my room.

I close my door and place the burning candle on the nightstand before lying down on the bed. Pulling the covers up to my chin, I stare at the flickering orange glow that the candle illuminates on to the ceiling.

It's too quiet in this room, so much so that my brain is allowed to run a million miles per hour. My mind wanders towards Tony-land. If I close my eyes and imagine just right, I can feel him lying here next to me. I remember how he comforted me after my mom died. If I try hard enough I can smell him, the smell of earth and soap. I can feel his strong arms wrapped around me, allowing me to feel safe and secure. I refuse to look to my left because if I do, I will see the empty bed. I'm doing so well at conjuring up the memory of Tony that I can almost hear him calling my name.

"*Willow.*" His voice echoes in my head gently, time after time.

With each time he calls my name, I feel myself slipping further and further from reality. "*I can't let myself do this, feel this. I need to face reality. That you are no longer you.*" I say as if I can speak directly to the Tony who is whispering my name inside my head.

"*Willow, I'm sorry. I didn't know this would happen so fast. When you told me what he'd done to me, I had no idea I could be taken over so easily. I almost hurt you. I can't let that happen again.*"

I gasp for air as I sit up quickly in my bed. I just heard Tony talking to me. Not Zack, Tony. "*Am I going crazy?*" I run my hands through my tangled curls.

"*You aren't crazy, Willow,*" he answers me.

I jump out of my bed and run barefooted to the window. Pushing back the curtains, I scan the dark tree line. "*Tony?*" I ask with a mixture of excitement and fear. The cocktail of emotions running through me is hard to understand.

I watch from a distance as he takes a step out of the shadows. The moonlight illuminates his figure. He's still too far away for me to see his eyes, but I recognize his silhouette instantly.

"I'm here, Willow." He holds his hand up.

"Is it you? I can't see your eyes," I ask, hopeful, yet afraid of his answer. It has to be him. Anytime Zack had control of Tony, the voice inside my head was Zack's.

"As far as I know, it's me." He puts his hand down but doesn't take another step in my direction.

"Wait there, I'll come down." I know it's probably the stupidest, most cliché move ever, but I have every intention of seeing Tony and trying to heal him again. *"Maybe if I try harder this time it will work."*

"No!" Tony's scream inside my head startles me. *"You aren't safe around me. Don't come down. I'll leave the second I no longer see you in that window. I can't chance being near you again..."* His voice trails off and I worry that he's already left. Then he speaks again. *"I'm so sorry I tried to hurt you, Willow. I don't know how I let that happen. How could I allow him to take over me like that?"*

"You had no choice, Tony. Zack did this to you. It's not your fault." I want so badly to run to him, but I believe it when he says that he will disappear the second I move from this window.

"I should be stronger!" I can hear the inner struggle in his thoughts.

I wish I could look into his eyes. Would they be yellow or red? *"You are strong, Tony. You fought it for a long time. If you just let me come down, I can try to heal you again. Maybe it'll work this time."*

Even from this distance, I can see him shaking his head. *"No, Willow,"* he says with conviction. *"You're not safe around me. I just came to tell you that you have to stay away from me. Don't try to find me."* I watch his hand move up to his hair. *"Most important of all, don't trust me. Ever! Promise me, Willow!"* he demands of me.

Something inside me breaks. How hard must it be for him to tell me this? *"I can't, Tony. I can't just sit here and do nothing. I have to try and help you."*

"NO!" This time his command is so loud it reverberates in my head. *"Stay away from me! I don't want you around me."*

His words sting. *"You don't want me?"* I know those aren't his exact words, but I can't help but single them out.

He doesn't answer for a moment. Finally he says, *"No, Willow. You need to move on. Don't come near me again."* His inner voice is monotone and emotionless.

I clutch my hand to my chest. *"You don't mean this, Tony!"* A thought pops into my head. *"Is that you, Zack? Are you taking over again?"* It's the only explanation. I try to convince myself of the lie. But deep down, I know its Tony, not Zack.

"No, it's me, Willow. I mean it. Stay away from me, please," he begs of me.

I shake my head as tears come to my eyes. Then as quickly as he appeared, he's gone. I look for any sign of him, but see nothing. *"Tony?"* I ask. *"Tony!"* I yell stronger. He doesn't answer me. *"Tony, please come back!"* Nothing.

I break down and crumple to the floor near the

window. How can he just leave me like that? How can he tell me that he doesn't want me around? He won't even give me the opportunity to try to help him.

I am too tired to cry. Instead, I curl up in a ball and fall asleep on the floor, thinking of Tony.

When the first rays of sun trickle in through the window above me, I wake up.

Realizing it's a little past dawn, I hastily get ready.

Most everyone is downstairs already when I arrive. Claire runs up to me and gives me a hug. "You still look so tired, Willow."

"You don't look so amazing yourself, Claire-Bear," I try to joke back but I can't quite bring a smile to my face. The wounds from last night's encounter with Tony are still too fresh.

She can see the weariness in my eyes and opens her mouth to say something, but she's distracted by her boyfriend, who's jogging towards us.

"Hey, babe. Hey, Willow." Connor captures us both in a big bear hug.

Claire giggles and I grunt. I missed this big old goofball.

I look around for Connor's parents and Lily. "Are your parents coming with us?"

He shakes his head. "No, they're going with Lee. They think it's what's best for Lily."

I make a mental note to tell Lee to keep an eye on them. I hope they won't turn into one of Zack's puppets, but they were part of the most recent group of people that we saved. "What do they think of you coming with us?" I ask him.

"Mom's not too happy about it. Dad wants to come with but that would break Lily's heart. I think he's secretly proud of me though." Connor smiles, then adds, "I'm ready to kick some bad guy butt!"

Claire hits him in the side jokingly. "Don't you mean *we* are ready?"

Connor looks down at Claire, who is so petite and fragile-looking when standing next to him. "Uh-huh. That's what I meant, babe."

I laugh, which surprises me. I didn't know I had it in me this morning.

"It's a good thing you're cute," she says to Connor.

He winks at her, and then leans in for a kiss. That's my cue to look away.

"Hey, Willow," Candy calls from behind me.

I turn to look at her. She wasn't around at all last night so I hadn't gotten a chance to check on her. Thankfully, her blue eyes are shining much brighter than the last time I saw her. I hope she's working through everything that has happened with her brother. "Hi, Candy."

"I heard he's still alive." She certainly doesn't beat around the bush. "I want to help you though. He may be my brother but I know now that he needs to be stopped."

I'm surprised that she wants to be involved. I had

assumed she would split off with Lee. I look behind her and see Jake only a few feet from her. He would be a good addition to our team, not that Candy wouldn't be. Her skills may come in handy. "Thank you, Candy...but, are you sure? I mean, I would completely understand if you wanted to go with Lee."

She shakes her head. "No, Willow. I need to do this. He's my blood and I feel responsible for helping to stop him."

"Okay." I relent since she's obviously given ample thought to this decision. "I'd be happy to have you on our team," I tell her.

She gives me a half smile and waves Jake over. He says a quick hello to me and then they both go to stand on our side of the room.

I notice then that everyone has begun dividing into two sections. Assumingly, one of them will be going with Lee and the other with me. In the middle of the room, a few people say their goodbyes.

I find my dad and Sabby in the middle. "Don't go, Wello," Sabby says as he reaches his hands up to me in the air, begging to be picked up.

I scoop him up into my arms and hug him tight. "I have to, buddy. Remember, secret mission?" I whisper into his ear.

He pulls back and nods his head. "I be brave, Wello," he tells me.

I wish he could just be a kid instead of having to be a brave four year old. "I know you will. Love you, bud." I kiss him on the cheek and then set him down.

His hand reaches up and wipes my kiss away from his face but he doesn't give me a grossed-out look. "I wuv you, too."

I purse my lips to contain my laugh and turn to my dad. "Be safe," he tells me.

"I will. You too." I try not to get emotional.

He pulls me into his arms. "I will never get tired of telling you that I'm proud of you. You are just like your mom."

"Thanks Dad, that means a lot. I love you."

"Love you too, sweetie," he says one last time.

I give them another hug and, instead of saying goodbye, this time we tell each other, "I'll see you later."

Next, I find Lee, who is giving some directions to a group of soldiers.

He turns to look at me. "You don't look like you got much sleep last night, Willow."

I shrug my shoulders. "I must look hideous since I'm getting that a lot this morning."

He doesn't answer me. Instead, I follow Lee's eyes, which are looking just behind me. I turn to see Alec approaching.

He nods to me and then says, "Good morning, Lee."

"Morning." He looks from Alec to me as if asking me if he should continue talking in front of him.

"Yes, Alec will be one of my next-in-command now." It hurts knowing that, in a way, Tony is being replaced. Alec looks in my direction and a look of honor crosses his face. I can tell what I just said means a lot to him.

Lee doesn't look too surprised at my decision. With that out of the way, he begins his strategy session again. "We'll be going to a safe house about fifteen miles northeast from here. I know you wanted all of the people that we rescued recently to go with you, but I fear that they aren't trained enough for that. They'd be more of a liability than an asset. I'm sending the few that volunteered to go, but the number is minimal."

"You do understand that you have to be on the lookout for changes in them." I don't like the idea that we don't know who is at risk of being controlled by Zack. Especially not when my father and Sabby are put in possible harm's way.

He nods his head. "I understand. Their eyes will turn red, right? Any other signs?"

I shake my head. "To be honest, Tony's eyes only turned red for short periods of time. Basically only when Zack had control of him, then his eyes turned back to their normal color after the episode. In most cases, Tony didn't remember anything he did while being controlled." I think about his apology last night. Obviously, that is changing since he remembered chasing me. He never had an inkling of recollection after any of his previous episodes. That has to be the worst part for Tony, the feeling of helplessness, of being trapped. "I would just say to keep a close eye on the recent prisoners that we saved at all times. It didn't take long before Tony started exhibiting signs. I would think that you'll notice something change in the next day or so if it's going to happen."

"Do you think Zack can control more than one person at a time?" Alec asks.

I hadn't thought of that. If Zack literally had full control of Tony, so much so that he actually controlled his thoughts and I could hear his voice, then I doubt that he would be able to control another person at the same time. "I don't think so. But that's not saying anything. What if he has his other goons controlling people while he personally keeps Tony in check?" Except, he didn't have control of him last night. I wonder what he was doing then.

"That's twisted," Alec declares.

I agree full heartedly. "Yep."

Lee continues with his debriefing. "In addition, I have a team going back to the prison. They had electricity back there and I believe they may have other forms of communication available to us. Our hope is that Zack has abandoned that station. If we can get inside safely, we have plans to try and make contact with F.E.M.A. or the D.O.D."

My eyes widen. Like wheels in motion, my brain starts processing what he's implying. With everything that has happened, I haven't really had time to think about the other shelters, the rest of the world. With no electricity or means of communication, our world got a whole lot smaller out here. What is going on in the other shelters? Do they know that Project ELE didn't work? Will they come out of this with powers as well?

"The D.O.D.?" I ask, not sure who they are.

"The Department of Defense." He lowers his voice so it won't travel much further than Alec and me. "We've uncovered some fishy stuff over the past few days. A man we rescued was familiar with one of Zack's henchmen. He said that the man's name is Derrick and that he served in the Army with him. Apparently, Derrick had been promoted into a very secretive Special Forces unit not too long ago. We don't have much more information than that, but this tells me that Zack's people aren't small potatoes."

I think about everything that went down outside the shelter. "You're right. How else would he get his hands on helicopters, vehicles, and electricity?" I can't believe I hadn't questioned this further before now. I guess it had something to do with just trying to keep my head above water.

Lee puts his finger to his lips, reminding me to keep it down. Chances are high that if people see me panic, it'll start a chain reaction.

Alec chimes in. "I get that, but how can the government not know what's going on here? Wouldn't they know that one of their shelters basically blew up?"

Lee nods his head. "Exactly. They have to know what's going on, or at least a part of it. I want to know why they haven't stepped in. That's why we have to find a way to make contact. If we make contact, they will be forced to recognize what's going on out here. They won't be able to ignore us any longer."

"Do you think that the people in the other shelters have powers like us?" I ask.

38

"I don't know. For our future's sake, I hope not. I can't imagine a world where everyone possesses these powers," Lee answers.

I think that no matter what, this world will never be the same. We fall silent for a second, each of us lost in our own thoughts.

"Are you ready?" Lee asks.

"Yes, I am," I tell him. "Good luck."

"Good luck to you too, Willow," he tells media can see the pain in his eyes…like he's scared of leaving media watch him take a deep breath and he gives me a slight nod. I guess he's come to terms with needing to let me go out on my own.

We shake hands and then go to our respective sides of the room. I can't help but notice that the number of people on my side is much less than Lee's. I feel better about that though, less people to be responsible for.

I hear Lee speaking to the group behind me. He gives a short hoo-rah speech that has everyone clapping in the end. I turn around and watch as the hordes of people exit the room.

I look back at our group who is left in this cavernous dining hall. Everyone seems to have their gear ready to go. They look to me for further direction. Alec nudges me lightly and whispers, "Don't you think it's time for a speech?" He laughs when I groan.

"I really don't enjoy public speaking," I complain to Alec.

He smiles at me and in that smile, I see our

friendship at work. A few puzzle pieces have been pieced together overnight, I guess. "I know, but you're good at it. They look up to you," he states, giving me the reassurance I needed.

I'm only sixteen, not necessarily an age that deserves much respect. Even still, I know my mom saw something in me and so did all of the people who nominated me to take charge. It's her legacy that she leaves behind that urges me to carry on. I want to know that if she were still here, I would make her proud. I reach down and touch the pocket of my jeans, feeling her final words tucked securely inside.

I look around at everyone on my team. The number isn't impressive by any means. I count thirty-three people on our side. Since I hate odd numbers, I decide to add myself in the mix to make it thirty-four. I know pretty much everyone on my team. I notice Marya, the girl I met who has telekinesis. A man, who looks to be twenty or so, with bright yellow eyes, is standing close to her. He possesses the same strawberry-blonde hair and good looks as she does. I can only assume that he's the cousin that saved her.

I scan the rest of the group and end up locking eyes with Jennifer. She stares at me with her untrusting, silvery-grey eyes. When I first met her, she looked much older than she does today. Her hair has been pulled over her shoulder and secured in a braid. She tied a small piece of ribbon to the bottom, giving her a child-like quality. She looks to be the same age as Marya, around seventeen or so. I haven't yet figured out what powers those grey eyes hold.

I can only guess that they provide some sort of shield since nothing I did worked on her back in the maze.

I take a deep breath and clear my throat loud enough to gain everyone's attention. It takes a few tries but eventually everyone quiets down. I look around the area at each one of my team member's faces. I pin them to memory, knowing that if anything happens to any one of them, it'll fall back on my shoulders. Without the safety net Lee provided me before, I feel naked and insecure. Leading a group of this size, even if it's considered small, sets me at unease. I begin questioning my motives and quickly resolve all the negativity. I have to remain focused and positive… it's what my mother would have done. I stifle a small cry in her memory and address the individuals standing before me.

"I want to thank each and every one of you for being here with me today. You don't know how much it means to me to know that we share the same vision. We all share the desire to bring Zack Hastings to his knees and to take down his minions too. The risks are great and the road will be tough, but I know deep down that all of you possess the strength needed to survive this journey. As God is my witness, I pledge to do everything in my power to bring each and every one of you home to safety. In order to do this I need us to stick together and never lack in communication. It is essential that each one of us knows exactly what's going on at all times. The odds are against us, as you already know. There are Reapers lurking in the shadows and people we will run into whose loyalties lay elsewhere. Never underestimate Zack's hold on his men. They have been brainwashed into believing that Zack's vision for power is one that will enable them to take complete control over the area…and possibly over the world. "I have no idea where the speech emanated from; possibly my mother gave me the words. I can tell by the faces of the people on my team that I have won them over. They are ready for whatever life throws their way.

"The proposal we have is one of simplicity. We plan on hiding out in a central location while sending out teams to scout the area. If we have any hope of beating Zack at his game, it will be that we have outsmarted him. We have to think critically and intelligently. We have to work together. Each of your opinions count, more than you'll ever know. One of us could hold the key to bringing down Zack and his army. If we keep our values in place, we should have no problem beating Zack at his own game. "I finish my speech.

The silence in the room is deafening. One could hear a single pin drop. Then, when I think I've lost everyone, a single clap emanates from the back of the room. I notice that it's started by Connor but the point is that it's followed by another and another until the entire room is enveloped in applause. A smile etches itself across my face. I try to suppress it but am unable to do so.

I feel Alec placing his arm around my shoulder and he gives it a squeeze. "Your mom would be so proud," he says to me so quietly that I'm the only one who can hear it.

This time, at the mention of my mother, I no longer

feel sad. I feel blessed. Blessed that I am the one chosen to carry on her legacy. Blessed that she made me believe in myself and made me into the person I am today. I would be nothing without her. "I love you, Mom," I whisper into the air. Hoping it will drift until it reaches her…wherever she is.

◎◎

We take to the woods like a fish takes to water. Each of us is on high alert as we head back towards the mountain. It's a long shot but I'm hoping to enlist the help of some acquaintances for our mission. That is, if they don't send us away immediately. Our reception the first time we met wasn't the most welcoming one.

As the mountain comes into view off in the distance, thoughts of Reapers cloud my vision. I find it especially odd that they've seemed to disappear altogether. As if they've never existed. Could they be lurking in the woods closer to the mountain?

After a few hours of walking in hushed silence, Claire trots up to my side, along with Connor. "Hey, Willow," she says, linking her arm in mine.

"Hey, Claire," I answer, patting her hand. She hesitates for a moment, cluing me in that she has something on her mind that she wants to tell me. "Spit it out," I say to her playfully.

She feigns hurt and puts her hand to her heart. "Willow, why would you think I had something on my mind?"

I laugh, answering her question. "I just know you."

She smiles up at me. "Well, okay. I did have something to ask you. "She hesitates for a moment before asking. "Is it going to be hard for you going after Zack like this? I mean, Tony is bound to come into the picture sooner or later if Zack has control over him. How are you going to handle that? If push comes to shove, will you have the strength to fight him?"

I knew the question would be brought up sooner rather than later. I just didn't expect Claire to be the one to do it. "I don't know. I'm not going to say it'll be easy, because that would be a complete lie. But, I'll deal with it when it happens."

"Don't worry, if he tries to hurt you, Alec and I will be right there to defend you." Connor slaps me on the shoulder lightly.

His words don't comfort me in the least. The thought of someone hurting Tony brings out the protective instincts within me. I don't want anything bad to happen to him. Well, at least nothing worse than what has already occurred. "I don't want anyone hurting Tony. You can subdue him if need be, but please don't hurt him. He's still good. He hasn't lost complete touch with reality." I fail to mention the fact that Tony is much stronger than the two of them combined, so good luck with that.

"How can you possibly know that, Willow? Didn't he try to kill you?" I hadn't realized that Alec had entered in on our quiet conversation until now. Last I saw, he was in the back of the group making sure everyone was keeping pace. We lock eyes and I can see the anger in them as well as the protective instincts he feels towards me.

I answer him assuredly. "I know because we talked last night."

"What?" Alec says all too loudly, drawing unwanted attention.

I shush him and look back at the people behind us. They look at us with interest. I make my voice even quieter now that they're aware of our conversation. "I could hear him from the woods. I stayed in my room. He didn't come any closer than the tree line and he only stayed for a few minutes. He apologized for chasing me. He has no control of himself when Zack takes over."

"What do you mean you could hear him?" Claire asks. I cringe, realizing I'm now going to have to divulge our secret.

I can't help looking at Alec when I answer. He doesn't look happy at all. "We don't fully understand the why of it, but for some reason, Tony and I can speak to each other through our minds."

Alec does a horrible job of trying to mask his hurt.

"I'm sorry," I try to say in my mind to him. Of course, he doesn't hear me. Would it be easier if he did? If what Tony and I share is something that I can share with anyone I wish...if it wasn't special?

Connor looks intrigued and says, "That is so cool. Can you do it with me?" He closes his mouth and gives me an intense look, that borderlines a creepy, serial-killer glare. When I don't answer him, he moves his face closer to me, leaving only two inches between us.

I reach my hand up between us and gently push his face away with the palm of my hand. "Um, no. I don't think it works that way. In fact, I've never been able to speak to someone and have them hear me. I can hear your thoughts, if I want to of course, since that's my original gift, but I can't send my thoughts to you. I don't know why I am able to do that with Tony."

Claire senses the tension between Alec and me, so she politely changes the subject. "Do you think that Erik and his people will be able to help us?"

"I hope so, since we're almost there. If not, at least they can provide us shelter for a day or two," I answer.

We see a break in the woods not far ahead. I motion for everyone to stay quiet as we come upon the paved road. Just like the last time, it's eerily quiet.

We follow the road, sticking close to the tree line, ready to take shelter if need be. Soon, we make out the grouping of scattered log cabins up ahead. We walk under the arch that holds the sign declaring this place: Camp Cheley.

From what I can see, there is no sign of life. That's not much to go on though, since the first time we came everyone did a great job of hiding. I wonder though, if they abandoned this place after everything went down at the shelter.

We walk up to the main building that they call: The Commons. I put my hands up in the air and motion for everyone else to do the same. "Erik?" I call out. "We mean no harm." A minute passes with no sign at all that this camp is still occupied.

"Nobody's home," Connor says.

I turn and glare at him. "Quiet."

We wait in silence and allow another two minutes or so to pass. That's when I hear the distinct sound of ammo being chambered into a shotgun behind us.

I turn, keeping my hands in the air, to find that we've been completely surrounded. I look at the intimidating number of people that hold a wide variety of weapons. Thankfully, I don't see any red eyes among the crowd.

"What do you want?" demands a dark-haired, intimidating man in the middle of the group, who towers over six feet in height. Back in the day when sports were popular, he would have made a great basketball player. The most notable thing about him is the awesome pair of blacked-out aviator sunglasses he's sporting. With the overcast sky today, it's hardly needed, but they definitely make him look like a boss. When I breathe a sharp intake of air, he points his gun right at me, causing my palms to become a clammy mess.

I open my mouth to ask for Erik but Alec steps in front of me. "Hey, Morgan!"

Morgan turns his ear towards Alec. The hard set of his facial features seems to lighten just a tad.

"Alec, my man, long time no see." He gives off a short laugh, as does Alec. He seems to relax slightly but he doesn't drop his weapon. His voice is still intimidating as he asks, "What exactly are you doing here?"

"We're looking for some help. Did you hear about what happened at the shelter?" Alec is smart enough not to move forward or drop his hands while he talks to Morgan.

I can see the posture of those holding weapons stiffen at the mention of the incident. Morgan answers somberly. "Yes. We heard of it. Many of the refugees are still with us. We heard about the number of people who were killed as well. That *they* took their bodies." He shakes his head in disgust.

"Yes, some were killed. But, there is a lot more to the story than meets the eye. The people who were shot were not automatically killed. They were shot with tranquilizers to subdue them. We fear that there is a greater conspiracy at work here than our group is prepared to take on alone. We would like to meet with Erik about this matter as soon as possible," Alec says.

Alec has the natural qualities of a leader. He used to be my boss after all, so he doesn't lack experience. The tone of voice he uses can calm any situation and put the most anxious of people at ease. I wonder if things were different, would he be the one leading our people instead of me?

Morgan speaks to one of his men in a volume meant to keep us from listening. We allow him a few seconds before he answers. "We will take you to Erik, but the rest of the group must stay here under our watch until Erik says otherwise."

I open my mouth to make an objection, but Alec does it for me. "I will come with you but I also request that you allow me to bring our leader with us to meet with Erik."

Morgan looks at Alec. "Are you not their leader?"
Alec shakes his head and smiles. "No."
"Then who is?" Morgan asks.
Alec gestures to me. "This is Willow Mosby, the leader of our team."
A man to his left whispers in his ear. Then, both he and Morgan laugh. Not just a normal laugh either, a bountiful, belly-shaking laugh. The rest of their group joins in as if they all heard this inside joke. "She's a babe," Morgan says with humor.

Embarrassed and a bit peeved, I drop my hands and place them on my hips. "Excuse me?" Some of the men tense at my sudden movement, so I put my hands in the air again. "I don't see what my looks have to do with my ability to effectively lead these people."

Morgan laughs again. My cheeks heat and I give him a heated, fiery glare as he takes such obvious amusement in me. I wish he would take off those stupid glasses so we can meet eye to eye. I have to force myself not to unleash the wrath of my powers on him to show just how capable I am. Don't think the thought of uprooting a tree or snatching those sunglasses off his face hasn't crossed my mind.

He holds up his hands as if to keep me from getting more upset. "Don't get me wrong, they say you are cute and all but..." He has to stifle another fit of laughter. "I meant that you are young, like a baby...babe..." He holds his side with his free hand as if his fit of laughter caused him pain.

"Oh," I say. Understanding his meaning doesn't

make it any less mortifying. "Well, I am sixteen years old and I fully expect that you will allow me to accompany Alec to speak with Erik. He knows of me and would not be happy if you kept me from meeting with him." I stand up as tall as I can, lengthening my spine.

The man next to him whispers in his ear again. I really wish I could hear what they are saying. I try to read their minds but it's to no avail. A hint of amusement flashes across Morgan's face. He waves his hand at us. "Very well then. You two, come with me."

I roll my eyes and take the lead in front of Alec, heading towards Morgan. His men take special care not to point their guns directly at us as we approach.

Alec immediately holds his hand out and he and Morgan do that manly handshake-half hug thing that guys do. Is this what they rehearse on a guy's night out? Alec steps aside and gives me a look that I can't quite interpret.

Morgan holds his hand out towards me. I shake his hand and the instant our hands touch, he audibly takes a breath. The men next to him tense. I look at Morgan with surprise. I can't see anything past the black lenses of his glasses. They are so opaquely dark that I have no idea how he can actually see through them. He holds on to my hand a little too long, making me feel uncomfortable. Finally, he lets go of my hand and smiles at me. "It's nice to meet you, Willow."

"Nice to meet you too." I have to force myself not to wipe my hand on my pants. It's not that his hands were sweaty or gross by any means, it's just that the whole greeting has me a bit weirded out. I hate that my hands get clammy, that's no quality for a leader to have.

With the introductions out of the way, Morgan turns around. Someone hands him a small, black, stick-looking thing. With a flick of a wrist, he turns it into a long cane. I look at Alec and then back to Morgan as we begin walking around our group, towards the entrance to The Commons. Morgan uses the cane to guide himself.

Is he blind?

Morgan's men don't follow us. They stay behind to keep an eye on our group. When we reach the door to The Commons, it opens automatically. Like before, I see the invisible man with purple eyes standing behind it. I wonder if he's their permanent doorman, seeing as how he was here the last time we came.

"We'll wait in our meeting room for Erik." Morgan directs us to the same room I waited in last time. I take a seat in one of the swivel chairs. I can't help but feel the weight that comes with seeing the empty chairs to my left. The ones that my mom and Tony sat in the last time we were here. I take a deep breath, exhaling through the painful memories.

As if reading my feelings, Alec sits to my right and puts his hand gently on my knee. I give him a weak smile.

Morgan calls to someone in the hall. "Please have Erik meet us in here at his earliest convenience."

"Yes sir." I hear a woman call back.

Morgan enters the room and closes the door behind him. He takes a seat on the other side of the table across from me. Using both of his hands, he pushes the cane in on itself, making it only about six inches long. He sets it on top of the table to his right and places both of his hands above the table in a steeple position. "You are a very special woman, Willow."

I look at him strangely and then look to Alec, who has an amused expression on his face. "Thank you," I say to Morgan.

He removes his sunglasses. He keeps his eyes closed for a second before he slowly opens them.

I gasp in shock as I look into his eyes. Alec gently squeezes my knee as if saying it's okay. Morgan's eyes lack almost all pigmentation. His black pupils stand out in stark contrast to his white irises. Only when I look closely enough can I tell that there is a slight difference between the iris and the sclera. I've never seen anything like it. I'm stunned speechless.

Morgan puts his sunglasses on again. I hate to admit that it makes me feel a little more at ease with him. I chide myself because different is not bad. I'm just not used to seeing anyone with eyes like that. I shiver as I wonder what in the world that color can mean.

"I'm a reader," he says as if reading the question that floats in the air. "From what I've seen in you, it won't be long before you're one too."

I blink a few times but have a hard time finding the right words. I have so many questions about this new ability. "Will I be blind too?" I instantly feel guilty that this was the first question that came blubbering from my mouth.

Not seeming bothered by it, he shrugs his shoulders. "I don't know. From what I've seen of your other abilities, I think that the loss of sight will affect you only when you use the gift."

"Were you blind before?" I ask.

He shakes his head. "No, it came on as suddenly as the gift did. I guess it was good that we left the shelter lines at nighttime."

"Huh?" I ask, not understanding what that has to do with anything.

He leans back in his chair and crosses his legs. "I guess since you will be able to read me soon anyway, I might as well tell you the whole story." He gives me an amused smile. "It will be nice having someone around with my same gift. I haven't run into any others yet... Anyhow, I digress... My brothers are the only family I have left. Much like you, it wasn't until I took the immunization that I realized that one of my brothers was declined."

My mouth drops open. "How did you know?" I shiver, remembering the moment when I saw the declined stamp on Sabby's passport.

He leans towards me and lowers his glasses just enough for me to see his white eyes again. "Reader, remember?" he says before using his index finger to push his glasses back up on the bridge of his nose.

"Yes, I'm sorry," I say even though I still haven't gotten all of the details of what a Reader does.

"So, I was saying... My younger brother, Seth, was

not accepted. Erik and I made the choice at that time to take Seth and fend for ourselves on the outside."

I connect the dots. "You're Erik's brother?"

He shifts in his seat. "Yes."

"Are you the one that left Molly in the woods?" I think back to the girl that we saved, the one that brought us here in the first place. She had yelled at Erik and told him that his brother left her there, defenseless against the Reapers.

He shakes his head and sighs. "No. Unfortunately, that was my brother Seth. He has some responsibility issues that we are working through."

"Oh, good," I say. Hopefully, Seth has worked through it and apologized to her profusely.

He thrums his hands against the table before continuing. "This is a long story, Willow. Are you going to let me tell it or are you going to keep interrupting me?"

My cheeks flush with embarrassment. "Yes, I'm sorry," I say again.

"Thank you." He gives me a humorous smile that tells me that he's not nearly as annoyed by my questions as he's letting on. I relax as he continues. "They didn't want to let Erik and me leave. We basically had to fight our way out of the testing station. That's how we got our first gun. We didn't shoot anyone, but we did have to do a lot of threatening to get by the officials. I didn't think we were going to make it out of the station alive but a doctor, who must have had a lot of authority, came out of the shelter and told the officials to let us go. It was really odd because the doctor looked right at me that night and told me that I'd better not make him regret this and that I better stay alive." Morgan runs his hands through his dark brown hair before he continues. "There were a lot of other rejects outside the shelter's perimeter that night. Since my brothers and I used to go to this camp every year as boys, we decided to set up camp here. Erik offered the other rejects the option to come with us. That's how my brother became their leader. This all happened at night. The following morning when I went outside, the sun was shining brightly in the sky. I remember there wasn't a cloud in sight that day, just a beautiful endless, blue sky. Within an hour, I was struck blind."

I can feel the emotions running off him. The fear he had when he couldn't see, the depression when he realized it was permanent, then the wonderment when he experienced his gift. Above all of the feelings, I feel a powerful sense of love and gratefulness. "You were struck blind but yet you still get to see the things you love most. Through the person you love," I whisper in awe.

He turns to me in surprise and nods his head slowly. "I forget that you have Erik's gift too. You can feel my emotions." He smiles wistfully. "Yes, I still get to see the things I love most. All I have to do is take my wife's hand and she shows it to me."

My heart warms. What an amazing love story. I want to ask him about her, but I'm hesitant to change the subject again... "How does your power work?"

"With a single touch I can see everything you've seen,

felt, been through. You name it, I read it." He rubs his chin with his thumb and index finger as if deciding whether he should add something. Thankfully, he does. "I know that you have been through a lot, Willow. I also know that you have so many different gifts but you still don't understand completely how you have obtained them." He puts both of his hands on the table and leans towards me. "Would you like to know the answer?"

My eyes widen as I stare at him. Do I want to know? If I know, will someone be able to replicate it? I look to Alec.

"It's up to you, Willow," he says as if he can read my thoughts. He sits back in the chair and crosses his left foot over his right knee.

I nod my head and then remember that Morgan can't see me. "Yes, please."

"I'm not going to tell you anything that you haven't already guessed. You injected just enough of the red shot to obtain the power that a Reaper has. Just like you thought, you *are* able to reap abilities, but you don't take everything from the person, just the right dose. You are nothing like the Reapers you've seen. You are a very powerful, yet grounded, young woman who cares deeply." He smiles and adds, "Your mother would be very proud of you."

A tear slips from my eyes as I hear his words. I let out the breath that I'd been holding. It's a relief to finally hear the answers. In the back of my mind, I had always wondered if one day I would lose touch with my humanity and become a full-blooded Reaper. To know that this won't happen removes a heavy burden from my shoulders. "Thank you," I tell him. "Please don't share this with anyone else," I add.

"I agree with your fears. This knowledge is not meant for the world to know. The last thing we need is for your type of powers to fall into the wrong hands. I will make sure that my brother and our people help you stop Zack. He can't be allowed to continue down this path."

"Thank you," I say, relieved.

"You are most welcome." He smiles and changes the subject. "So you can read minds, huh?"

I nod my head again, and then I roll my eyes. *He can't see you!* I try to etch it into my brain. "Yes, I can."

"Can you read mine now?" he asks with an amused expression.

"Um, yeah I can. Do you want me to?" I ask, confused.

He nods his head. "I just wanted to see how well it works. I haven't run into any mind readers yet."

"Okay..." I say a little uncertainly. I close my eyes and focus on opening up that channel that lets me read thoughts. I hear him so instantly that it startles me.

"I thought that you should know that Alec's love for you still runs very deep. He is trying his best to be your friend but it's hard for him. He's a very good man. I know that you have a kind heart. Tread lightly with him. In time you two will be able to rekindle your friendship..." I see his eyebrows rise up over his glasses. *"Act like I just said something funny. Tell him I told you that now that I've seen you that I think you are a*

real babe."

I laugh nervously and close down that gift. I turn to look at Alec, who is watching us curiously. "He said that I am a babe."

Alec laughs, but his eyes still hold that warmth towards me. "Yes, you are."

I look away shyly. "Yeah, but I bet your wife is a bigger babe," I tell Morgan.

"She's hotness personified." Morgan smiles like a man in love should.

That earns a laugh from Alec and me.

A knock sounds on the door and a second later Erik peeps in. He smiles and his black eyes light up when he sees me sitting next to Alec. "You found your man, I see!"

The humor we found a moment ago trickles away. Erik notices it too, or feels it with his gifts. "Oh." He holds his index finger up. "Just a moment." He backs out of the room and closes the door.

I raise my eyebrow in question at his weird behavior. Morgan laughs and Alec sits there quietly. I wonder if there will ever be a time in which this won't be a sore subject. *Give it time,* I remind myself of Morgan's words.

Erik knocks on the door and opens it again. He has a grin on his face as he says, "Willow, Alec! I'm so glad to see you. It's been a while and I've been wondering what had become of you two." I can't help but raise my eyebrow even higher at him. He rolls his eyes. "It wasn't any better, was it?"

I shake my head and laugh at his absurdity. Alec

does too, which breaks a layer of the icy tension in the room. "It's good to see you too, Erik," I say.

"So your theory on pressing that rewind button didn't work, did it?" Morgan pokes fun at his slightly younger brother.

Erik hangs his head in mock shame. "Not for me at least. If only I were like Willow. I'd have picked up on the coolest gift ever by now."

"What is the coolest gift ever?" I ask, even though I can think of quite a few that top the list.

He drops the shame act and takes a seat. "I call it rewinding. Well, I guess then I'd have to call it fast-forwarding too..."

"In English, please," Alec jokes with him.

This doesn't bother Erik in the least. I realize now that both brothers are quite fond of Alec. He couldn't have been in their presence for more than a day before he left them the last time. He just has that charismatic quality about him that makes everyone like him.

Erik answers. "The ability to move backwards and forwards through time. Like in a song or a movie where you can rewind and fast-forward to the parts you want to listen to or see. It's by far the coolest thing ever. Quite rare too, as I've only seen one person with the gift."

My curiosity is peeked. The things I could do if I were able to rewind and fast-forward through time. Could I save my mom? Stop Tony from being injected with that shot? "Is the person still here?"

Erik senses my emotions and says, "No, she left.

We thought it would be best to send Virginia away for a little while."

"Oh," I say, not quite getting his point.

Alec questions him. "What do you mean? Why would you send her away?"

Erik looks from Alec to me. "We have a person with sight here who has reason to believe that this wouldn't be the best gift for Willow to acquire at this time."

Shock and frustration sucker punches me in the chest. "What exactly are you getting at, Erik?" I don't hide the wounded pride from my voice or body language.

He moves in closer. His face takes on a gentle expression. I can see right through him as he tries to use his abilities to calm my escalating emotions.

I stand up so quickly that my chair falls down behind me. I put my hand up as if to block him. "Don't you dare try that on me! I asked you a question." My blood starts pumping. I don't like the idea that someone would have to be protected from me. That they would know what gifts I should or shouldn't 'acquire.'

Both Alec and Erik stare at me in awe. In the silence, Morgan grabs Erik's hand and a moment later mouths the word, "wow."

I glare at them and ask, "What are you ogling at?" I don't have to wait for their answer because I catch my reflection in a mirror near the door. I walk up closer to examine my eyes. They are a striking mixture of grey and silver. Just like Jennifer's, except for the red fleck that never fades from my irises.

"What did you just do?" Erik asks curiously.

I force myself to calm down. *I'm not mad at Erik*, I tell myself as I take a seat. Avoiding his question, I ask, "Do you not have anyone here with silver eyes?"

He shakes his head. "I would imagine that this color must be just as unique as Virginia's."

"What color were her eyes?" I ask.

"The lightest shade of green I've ever seen in someone's eyes. If I were to describe their exact color, I would say that they are the color of sea foam," Erik tells me.

I can imagine the light, minty green in my mind. I decide to answer his original question. "I don't know enough about the gift I get when my eyes turn this color. I barely know the girl who has this same gift and I imagine that she knows as little about her abilities as I do."

Morgan raises his index finger, asking permission to interrupt. "I saw the girl, Jennifer, when I read you. I believe she has a gift that I can only describe as a shield. She can block gifts if she wants to and allow others to affect her when it serves her purpose. I was intrigued when I saw that particular memory. I thought about inviting her in immediately, in hopes that she would offer me her hand. But, by your memory, she seems to be quite closed off. I doubt she would be willing to drop her shield in order for me to get an effective reading."

"Hmm. A shield. That is a good way of describing her gift," I tell him. Then I turn my sights back to Erik. "Okay, enough side talk, I want to know why you think I shouldn't be around this Virginia girl."

Erik laughs at my bluntness. "I would hardly call Virginia a girl. She has to be close to eighty years in age."

I scowl at him. "Erik..." I warn.

He puts both of his hands up in mock surrender. His face turns somber as he answers me. "Okay, okay. Look... It's not a pretty story. Our seer saw what would happen if you obtained the gift to move through time. It wasn't good, Willow. I am sure you didn't mean to, but you hurt a lot of people when you tried to prevent certain events from unfolding. You can't rewrite history without major consequences."

I look down. *Could I have really done that?* I know immediately that yes, I could very easily have done what the seer foretold. Did I not just have the thoughts of saving my mom and Tony? If I had the means, I would have acted on them without question.

Alec puts his hand on my back and rubs it gently. He leans in and whispers in my ear, "I know you wouldn't have done anything intentionally."

I look at him with sad eyes. "Thank you." I turn back to Erik. "You're right in keeping me from her. I'm sorry that I failed in that test."

Erik shakes his head. "It's not a test, Willow. This is life. You are human, for goodness sakes. You are what sixteen, seventeen? You are bound to make mistakes. We just had the opportunity to prevent this particular one from happening."

I still feel a bit down on myself at not being responsible enough to handle that ability. Erik is right though; I'm not perfect. In fact, if the world depended on my perfection, we'd all be in for a heaping of trouble. I decide to acknowledge this fact and move on. "Thank you, Erik." I run my hand through my messy curls and sit taller in my seat. "I've come here to ask for your help."

"You will have my full support, Willow. I already know what you wish from me and I agree full heartedly that Zack Hastings must be stopped," Erik answers before I can continue with my intended spiel.

"Well, thank you." I breathe out a sigh of relief before a thought pops into my mind. "Was that seer able to view the outcome of our mission?" I have not yet been able to take control with my gift of sight. I only get snapshots of future events here and there. They come to me randomly, without my requesting them.

He shakes his head. "I wish. Our seer did say that it would take a while. She saw the seasons change and a bitter cold take over while you were still here."

"A bitter cold?" asks Alec.

Morgan raises his hand as he answers for his brother. "Haven't you noticed the air turning crisp? This Project ELE has failed to bring upon the desired heating of our planet. Thank goodness." He laughs.

These people wouldn't have had the same type of protection as those who took the survival shot. If the earth had in fact heated beyond livable conditions, it would have made life unimaginably hard for everyone left outside. "If we are in for a long haul, I assume that you will okay my team staying with me?"

Erik stands up. "Yes, of course. They will become a great asset to our group. I will go make arrangements for you and your team to move in immediately."

I stand up and shake Erik's hand from across the table. "Thank you."

"You are very welcome." Erik smiles.

We follow him from the room and spend the remaining day getting settled in before dinner.

Camp Cheley is much bigger than it looks like from the outside.

Erik has spread our group out among the campus of log cabins. A few of us were assigned rooms in The Commons. Among my friends in The Commons, Alec and Connor share a room, Candy was paired with Marya, and I share a room with Claire.

After we wash the dirt off from our long hike through the woods, we head downstairs to meet back up with Erik. He offers to show us around. The Commons has a lot of the amenities that the Shelter offered. Unfortunately though, without electricity, most of them are useless. We walk by an Olympic-sized pool that has turned green from being unkempt.

Up ahead of me, I watch Connor nudge Alec in the side. "I dare you to jump in there."

Alec rolls his eyes. "How about you go first."

"You're no fun anymore," Connor chides. Alec laughs.

"Do you think we're safe out here?" Claire whispers to me.

"I do. Erik's people have managed to survive this

long amongst a forest filled with Reapers," I answer.

"You are all very safe here, young lady." I turn around to see Morgan following closely behind us. He is still sporting his iconic sunglasses. I didn't notice that he had joined the tour. He walks using the wall as a guide.

I stop. "This is my best friend Claire." I introduce her to Morgan.

"Nice to meet you, Claire. My name is Morgan." He holds his hand out for her.

She shakes his hand. I watch in amazement as he reads her. For a moment, his lips turn downward in a frown. Claire looks to me as if asking why the heck this man is still holding my hand. I look back at Morgan, who has started to smile again and is nodding his head. He releases her hand a second later.

"Um, what was that?" she asks me.

"Morgan is a reader. He can see your memories and basically read everything about you in a single touch," I answer.

She visibly shivers and storm clouds seem to roll in over her expression. I haven't seen Claire look like that since back in the shelter, before I had gotten to know her. I can feel her emotions running a gambit as she processes the fact that this man she just met now knows everything about her life.

"I'm sorry, I probably should have asked for your permission to do that," Morgan interjects.

"Yes, you probably should have." She runs her hands through her pale blonde hair and takes a deep breath as if she can exhale all of her feelings. Then she mouth's to me, "Is he blind?"

I nod my head.

"May I say that you have become a remarkable young woman despite your hardships." He looks slightly sad as he tells this to Claire.

She looks uncomfortable but manages to say, "Thank you."

I know that Claire has had a tough life since her parents died from the virus. I can't help feeling a bit jealous of Morgan though. He now knows my best friend more intimately than I do.

"Did you not meet Morgan the last time you were here?" I ask her.

"No, she was a little out of it at the time. Alec was the only one I really got the chance to interact with. Claire did meet my wife Audrey," Morgan answers for her.

"Oh, you're Audrey's husband!" Claire's face lights up. "She is amazing."

"That she is," Morgan agrees with a huge smile.

Claire looks at me. "I was a bit distraught when they found me and brought me here. After having been locked in that cavern and then seeing those Reapers when we first escaped, I sort of just shut down. It took me a while to process it. Audrey helped me a lot."

I nod my head in understanding. I totally get the shutting down part. I think back to when I first walked out of the shelter. I certainly wasn't ready to process everything that was happening in the world on the outside.

A tall, gorgeous woman, with dark, caramel skin and rich, dark hair comes bounding up behind Morgan. "I've been looking for you everywhere, babe!" she calls to him.

Morgan doesn't just smile at her voice; he beams brighter than the sun. She smiles at Claire and me as she approaches. Before introducing herself to us, she puts her hands in Morgan's. He continues to smile as he holds her hands tight. I feel a little awkward, like we are intruding on a very private moment.

"You weren't lying. You did look everywhere for me, sweetheart." He pulls her hand up to his lips and gives it a gentle kiss. Her copper eyes are filled with adoration for her husband.

She must be the seer. I can't help but wonder what she must think of me if she saw me hurt so many people upon coming in contact with Virginia's gift.

She turns to me, "I'm sorry, we are being rude. I'm Audrey and it's very nice to meet you, Willow." Her eyes hold no accusations, only kindness. She smiles at Claire, "I'm so happy to see you again, Claire."

Claire gives the woman a hug. "It's nice to see you again too, Audrey."

After hugging Claire, Audrey doesn't extend her hand to me. Instead, she pulls me into a hug. Part of me wants to consider it awkward but the other part of me takes comfort in this woman. She reminds me a little of my mom. Her eyes are kind and wise, yet she holds herself with a certain degree of authority and dignity.

"Nice to meet you," I tell her.

"Are you girl's hungry? I was just about to drag my husband off to the Mess Hall," she says.

"The Mess Hall?" I ask.

Morgan laughs. "Yes, it's where we all make a mess of ourselves as we grub out on food."

"Oh." My stomach growls at the mention of food.

"So you are hungry," he jokes.

I can't sustain the laugh that works its way up my throat. "Follow me," Audrey says. She takes her husband's hand into the crook of her arm and walks with him towards the Mess Hall. You can tell he has full trust in his wife because he doesn't walk timidly. He has full confidence, as if he can see the hall before him. Perhaps he actually can see it, through his wife's eyes.

As we enter the huge dining room – which is in fact labeled in childish block letters as The Mess Hall – we find Erik, Alec, and Connor. They must have circled around the facility because they are already in line for the buffet-style dinner.

Erik invites us to sit with his family. When I come to the table, I notice a familiar person sitting next to a man that looks like a younger version of Erik. Except this man, or boy, has neon-yellow eyes.

"Willow!" Molly jumps up from her seat and comes running towards me.

"Hi, Molly," I say not as enthusiastically, as I set my tray down. I like the girl, but last time she drove me a little nuts.

"I was hoping I'd see you again." She pulls my arm and jerks me around the table.

She looks at me excitedly with her bright purple eyes as she introduces the boy she was sitting next to. "This is my boyfriend, Seth!" She smiles giddily.

Seth wipes his mouth with his napkin before he stands up to greet me. "Nice to meet you," Seth says as he holds his hand out to me.

I shake his hand. "Nice to meet you too. I'm Willow."

"Yes, my brothers have told me about you." He lowers his voice and leans in to speak to me more intimately. "Thank you for taking care of Molly. I'm sorry that I left her like that. I had no idea I would react in such a way. I regret that day very much."

Molly, having heard his thank you, slaps him playfully on the arm. "Yeah, I make sure he never forgets it."

I chuckle. As much as I'd love to have given this boy a stern 'what for' because of his actions, I can see that Molly has probably made him pay for it tenfold. "You're welcome," I answer him.

I introduce Molly and Seth to my friends and then take a seat. I wave Candy and Jake over to our table after they make their way through the line. They sit on the opposite end as us. For the most part, they seem to keep more so to themselves as opposed to getting involved in our conversations. I can tell that they are really into each other.

I dig into the steaming hot meal of chicken and

dumplings. It is so freaking good that I'm sure I'm making embarrassing moaning and awing sounds as I shovel it into my mouth. I don't care though; having a warm meal really hits the spot.

After dinner, we meet with Erik and Morgan and hash out some basic plans. Since we don't know Zack's exact location, we'll have to send out a few surveillance teams. We set up a mission to check out the area west of the shelter. There have been reports of strange lights shining in the sky in that general vicinity. We figure that it's as good a start as any. In addition to our strategies to hunt Zack down, we make plans for our newest members to begin training. Some of the new arrivals that we have with us haven't been adequately trained. We nominate a few of Erik's men as well as mine to lead the defense training. We also set up for people with similar gifts to work together to sharpen each other's powers.

It feels good to take action and make plans. When I retire to my room with Claire, I find myself feeling exhausted, yet hopeful. Perhaps we can do this. We *can* take Zack down. I fall asleep easily and when I dream, I dream of Tony.

FIVE

I wake up when the first wisps of light filter into our room.

Taking advantage of being the first person up, I tiptoe to the bathroom and take a quick, cold shower. I'm towel drying my hair as I walk back into the room ten minutes later.

Claire is sitting Indian style on her bed. She's already fully dressed and ready to go. She smiles at me as I enter the room. "Good morning, sunshine."

"Good morning to you too. You seem like a happy camper this morning." I eye her, wondering why she looks so at peace.

She talks to me as she gathers her hair up into a high ponytail. "I know it may seem odd with us being in this strange place and about to head out into the battlefield and all, but it feels good to have all of my friends close by. You are like my sister and when you're gone, I miss you."

I hang the damp towel over a chair and walk to her side of the bed. "I've missed you too, Claire. I'm glad you are here with me. Oh, and as far as I'm concerned, we *are* sisters." I give her a quick hug.

Her eyes shine when we part. She sniffs and clears

her emotions from her face. "Okay, enough mushy-gushy this morning. I'm ready to kick some butt!" She hops out of bed.

I laugh and teasingly pull her ponytail as we walk out of the room.

Breakfast consists of quick protein bars and a bottle of water. I make my way down to the auditorium, which is next door to the Mess Hall. Alec, Connor, Candy, and Jake find us right away, amongst the throngs of people.

"You ready?" Alec asks me.

I nod my head. "Yes." I want to be excited about this mission but I can't help but remember what Erik said that Audrey saw. She didn't see us succeeding on this mission. I have to remember though, that any little bit of information that we find could lead to our success. Perhaps we won't find Zack or Tony today, but maybe we will get a few pieces of the puzzle.

Erik walks up the steps to stand on top of the small stage. He raises his voice and offers directions. "Thank you all for meeting with us this morning. As many of you have seen, we have some new faces at camp today." He finds my eyes in the crowd. "I have accepted the responsibility of helping Willow Mosby's people on their mission to stop the one's responsible for giving us these powers. I believe that her mission is one that will impact us all and this is why I've chosen to get involved when we have remained neutral previously. Those of you gathered here today will be split into two groups. I have already assigned each of you a number, which will tell you how you will be actively

73

participating in this operation."

"Group one will be going on the mission with us today to investigate the lights that were reported west of the shelter. We will need to be prepared for possible Reaper attacks during our journey. I ask that those of you with strength form the outermost perimeter of our group."

"Those of you in group two will be staying here and forming training sessions. Each of you have a special gift or power that I believe you have learned to master. You will be working with those left behind to develop their skills as well as help the remaining members of our team when we return. Group one, please gather your supplies and meet me outside in fifteen minutes. I want to thank everyone in advance for their participation."

He walks off the stage and the crowd disperses. Since we have already prepared our supplies, we are the first outside. Twenty people from my team stand around me. We have asked the newest survivors, who we saved, to stay behind to learn. That's why I'm surprised when I see Marya, standing tall, next to her cousin.

She notices me eyeing her immediately and approaches. Her golden eyes are set with determination. "Good morning, Willow." She holds her hands up when I open my mouth. "Look, I can tell that you are surprised to see me here since I'm one of the newbies. I can't stay behind though. I don't do well with staying in the shadows while everyone else does the messy work. I am strong and I know that my gift will be extremely useful to this mission." She bites her lip. I can see through her tough-girl persona. She's really scared inside but she's not about to let me see any weakness. Her desire to go is so strong that it temporarily blurs my vision.

I wonder how someone that isn't much older than I am came to be so confident. I remember not long ago, fighting with my mom and Tony when they were trying to keep me from going on a mission. It would be hypocritical of me to deny her when I was in her place before. "You can come *if* you agree to follow our directions to a T," I tell her. I hold her gaze, making sure she's really willing to abide by these conditions.

She nods her head and keeps her composure, even though there is obvious excitement in her eyes. "I will, I promise."

Her cousin Joseph sees her excitement and approaches. I nod to him, and then continue addressing Marya. "Good. Now, has Joseph told you about the Reapers?"

Marya's eyes turn dark. Joseph answers for her. "I didn't have to tell her much about them. She witnessed their fury when she first escaped the shelter. Thankfully, her powers came on strong and quick that day." He looks at her with pride. "She took out four Reapers before they were immobilized by Dr. Hastings's device."

I smile at her. "That is quite a feat, Marya. Good job," I say, impressed.

She shivers slightly as she adds, "If I had seen them shoot me in my back, I would have been able to keep from being captured too."

I nod my head. "I have no doubt you would have been able to stop bullets."

The darkness starts to fade from her eyes and she smiles. "Yes, I suppose I could do that. I just have to see them coming first."

"I think Erik's ready for you, Willow," Alec says from behind me.

I turn around, acknowledging him. "Thanks. Have you met Marya and her cousin Joseph?"

Alec looks over my shoulder at Marya. For an instant, an interesting expression crosses his features. I don't know what to think of that look but just as quickly as it comes, it leaves. "I've seen them around, but we haven't been formally introduced," Alec says loud enough for them to hear.

Marya steps forward and introduces herself boldly. I leave them to their introductions and head out to find Erik.

I find him easily, at the front of the crowd. He goes over our plans for the mission. Even though I would like to take the lead like my mother did so many times before, I agree to stay in the middle of the pack. Once again, I'd be a huge liability if a Reaper got me. Plus, if Zack's men are present, it would be best if they don't see me right away.

After a few more instructions, we leave. It takes a little over an hour to get anywhere close to the shelter. My head feels a little dizzy as we walk through the forest towards the tree line that leads to the clearing. The thought of stepping foot into the place where one of my worst nightmares came true makes my stomach tighten. My vision blurs on the edges, but I shake it off and keep moving. I can't wimp out now. We have to pass by the shelter to get to the area where the lights were last seen.

We step out into the open and I come face to face with the mountain that once was my home. Its metal doors are still wide open and are tinged with black. Debris is littered around the clearing, making it look every bit like the war zone that it was. I can't help but wonder if anyone was left inside those doors. I do a double take when I look past the doorway into the blackened inner workings of the shelter. A pair of red eyes glares at me from the inside. A shiver runs up and down my body as I stare at it with wide eyes.

"Is that what I think it is?" Claire whispers in my ear.

I nod my head, unwilling to remove my gaze from the Reaper. As if it were a spider or some other equally scary thing, I don't want to let it out of my sight in fear that it will disappear and gain an advantage on us.

Erik must have noticed this too, because he stops our group by outstretching his arm. The soldiers on our outer perimeter arm their weapons, pointing their barrels towards the doors. The clicking sound of the ammunition loading makes me shiver.

He motions for the first rung of men to follow him. At first, I wonder why he's going after the Reaper. This isn't our mission, but then again, those eyes could actually belong to one of Zack's puppets.

The red eyes disappear from view as our people

approach quietly. They make it to the entry and carefully take their first step inside. I get an overwhelming sense of nausea as they move further into the dark shelter. I can no longer see them. I hold my breath, waiting for any sign that the coast is clear, or confirmation that this is Zack's new lair. What better place to hide than in the charred remains of the shelter he watched his father create?

I release my breath when a minute later, Erik steps out into the light. He motions with his hand for us to approach. We move swiftly towards the entrance. Claire inches closer to me as we walk over the threshold in silence. The musky smell of burnt wood mixed with the chemical odor of melted wires and plastic fills my nose. I try breathing through my mouth and end up gagging. The odor is so strong that I can taste it. Claire puts her hand on my shoulder, but doesn't say anything. I compose myself and pat her hand, letting her know I'm okay.

Up ahead, I can see that somehow a few lights have remained unscathed and are working. We walk down the dark hall that leads to the main common area. I can't see Erik up ahead because the hall is too narrow and only four of us can walk side by side at a time.

Our silence is broken by the first scream. It's so low and guttural that I know it was a man who made the noise. Every muscle in my body tenses as I push Claire behind me. "Get out!" I yell to her as another cry fills the room. Then it turns into utter chaos. Gunfire rings out in the small quarters. People turn around and run past me, nearly trampling me in the process. I give Claire a slight shove, to get her moving backwards. Connor pushes through the crowd that was behind us and grabs her hand. I watch them disappear as he pulls Claire into the wall.

Bodies push me towards the exit but I know that some of my people are still up ahead. As their leader, I can't leave them in there. I focus on allowing myself to become fluid. It takes longer than I anticipated because my heart is beating so quickly. By the time I am able to walk through the first person, I'm nearly at the shelter doors. I start running through the crowd, unhindered by their actual body mass, because I'm using the same gift Connor possesses. As I near the opening to the common area, I see Marya on the floor in an unconscious state. I pause to help her, but Alec swoops down and picks her up so quickly into his arms that I would think he has a different gift than just a healer. Knowing they are both headed towards safety, I start running further into the mess.

"Reapers!" I hear people yell as they run past me.

The tables are still strung about in the large, open common area. Some are burnt and half-standing, some are flipped upside down. Most of the chairs are halfway melted. People are running towards the exit, away from the threat up ahead. Five of our men, including Erik, are taking a last stand of sorts, shooting into the grouping of Reapers that are advancing out of the woodworks. I count twenty at least, and more running down the halls. To the left I can see the large, three-story, open shopping area where all of the offices were. At least thirty more Reapers are descending both sides of the burnt escalators. *They are living in here!*

They made this shelter and all of its burnt remains their home!

I see the lifeless bodies of some of our people on the floor. Anger for what these soulless monsters have done consumes me. I start trembling with fury as gold mixed with red begins clouding my vision. The escalators begin shaking, as does the large, hanging lights in the commons area. One by one, the light bulbs burst, thrusting the room further and further into darkness. Using my mind, I rip the skirt plate that forms the stairs of the escalator off. This sends the Reapers on it tumbling to the ground below. Tables float in the air and I begin heaving them at the group of monsters that have surrounded us.

Something tackles me from the side. I fall to the floor and my vision goes dark.

"Willow?" someone whispers to me. Not just anybody, Claire.

What is she doing here? I think to myself.

"Willow?" She shakes my arm.

She shouldn't be here. It isn't safe. I open my eyes and find myself standing outside in the bright sunlight. We are at the edge of the woods, just shy of the clearing that leads to the shelter. My entire team is still here, safe.

"Are you okay?" Claire asks me. She moves into my line of sight, blocking my view of the shelter.

I shake my head. That had to have been a vision. My heart is still pounding loudly in my chest. The smell of charred material is still pungently attacking my nostrils. I can taste the burnt air. I don't hesitate. I move swiftly through the crowd towards Erik.

Erik is directing his people to move into the clearing. "Stop!" I call to him.

He looks at me with surprise. His body goes on alert and his eyes look at me with worry. "What is it?" He can read and feel my emotions before I speak. He knows my panic, my terror, my absolute distress.

"You can't go in there. We need to leave now," I tell him. My heart is still beating double time so I find it hard to catch my breath. Alec comes up behind me and puts his hand on my back. I feel his healing power running through my veins.

Ignoring Alec, Erik asks. "Was it Zack's men? Did you see someone?"

"It was Reapers. They've taken over the shelter. I saw what will happen if we go in there, if we attempt to enter the shelter. Most of us won't come out. There are too many of them for us to take on. I saw..." My stomach rolls with sickness from the vision and it causes me to double over. I heave the contents of my breakfast onto the forest floor.

Alec rubs my back as I try to regain control of myself. He's saying something to Erik, but I can't focus in on it clearly because my stomach is revolting against me.

"We'll leave now. You did good, Willow. You did good," Erik murmurs soothingly, trying to help me calm down.

Finally, I stop dry heaving and straighten up. I wipe at my eyes and nose and gladly accept a bottle of water that one of Erik's men hands me. I take a few sips and then apologize. "I'm sorry, it was just... It was bad." I feel ashamed and embarrassed that I reacted in such a way. Throwing up isn't exactly a great leadership trait.

"I believe you, Willow. We'll leave now. I think it's best that we head back to camp as quickly as possible. We'll have to make arrangements to investigate the lights on another day when we have a larger team," he tells me.

I'm grateful for his understanding but also disappointed that we have to push our search back. However, safety is our number one priority. I think of my mom and know that's what she would say.

Turning quickly, we head back to the camp. We take a different, more complicated route to make sure that we aren't followed. We don't arrive back until the sun is starting to set.

At night, I retire to my room early. The events of today have left me emotionally drained. I curl my arms around my knees and allow myself to shed a few tears. What I saw was horrific. Having seen humans cause such pain, such death, is unimaginable. The monsters looked just like us, yet they were nothing like us.

The next day Erik and I hash out a larger plan to investigate the area to the west of the shelter. The trip will take longer because we will have to bypass the clearing to avoid running into any Reapers. We increase the number of soldiers going with us and head out just before lunch.

When we reach the general vicinity of the area where they saw the lights, we find no sign of life. All we find is an abandoned industrial yard. A few power lines seem to be working, which is strange. This must be where the light is coming from. As to who turned on the lights, we're still not sure. We search the grounds and come up empty.

I feel deflated as we head back to camp, again empty-handed. Erik assures me that we will continue our search. I don't talk much during dinner. I sit and eat, watching everyone else interacting. They don't feel as disappointed as I do at our failed mission.

Connor and Claire laugh and playfully jab at each other. Alec is sitting next to Marya across the table from me. He seems very interesting in whatever she is saying. I watch Morgan and Audrey holding hands and whispering sweet nothings to each other.

I am surrounded by people but I've never felt so alone. Every minute, every hour that Tony is being used by Zack, is torture to me. Can they not see that I die a little more each day that we're apart? I catch Erik staring at me from across the table and I look away. I guess he sees it since he has no choice. I'm sure the feelings roll off me towards him like the ocean's tide comes in at night.

After dinner, we meet with several of our team leaders and discuss some plans to search other areas. Erik wants to check around the prison. I remember Lee's mission and agree to Erik's idea. I doubt that Zack would go anywhere near that place, but perhaps I'll get a chance to see Lee. I could make sure my father and Sabby are still doing well.

We make plans to head out the following day.

SIX

My muscles are sore and I still feel emotionally drained when I wake up in the morning.

This past month had been so chock-full of missions and training that it passed by before I knew it. Our first missions to the prison came up empty. We went out in four teams: north, south, east, and west. Our missions were to scour around the old jail, where Zack had been just days before, in our perspective directional areas. Needless to say, when we all met back at the camp that afternoon, no one had anything worthwhile to bring to the table. It was as if Zack and his people had vanished. I figured that would be the case, but the most disappointing thing to me was that we didn't find Lee. Perhaps he hadn't gone to the prison yet or he had already come and gone. I wish though, that I had been able to confirm that my family was doing well.

After the second failed mission, Erik pulled out a map and divided it up into sections… fifty-two to be exact. It covered a twenty-mile radius of the area around the jail. With four teams covering one area each day, leaving two days off a week to rest. That gave us a four-week window—give or take a day–to complete. The further we went, the longer each mission took.

It had been a unanimous decision to use that method to patrol the area. Unfortunately, when the last day came and went with nothing so much as a footprint to report, everyone became restless and agitated. Frustrated with our failed mission, we decided to go back to the drawing board and meet again this morning to brainstorm about what to do next.

I get dressed and meander down the hall, lost in thought, thankful to be by myself. I curl my hands inside the cuff of my sweater. It's begun turning cold outside just like Audrey predicted. The leaves have already turned from yellow to orange to red. Now they've begun falling and filling the forest with their festive colors.

This past month has been excruciatingly lonely. I've found myself withdrawing from my friends as each day passed. Between planning, running missions, and training, I've had no time to spend with them. The aching in my chest hasn't lessened at all over the past four weeks. Last night Claire had curled up behind me and brushed my hair as I cried over Tony. I haven't heard from him, which could be a good thing I guess, but it's hard not knowing. I'm pretty sure now that I'm hopelessly in love with the man. What hurts the most is the fact that I may never be able to tell him this. *Has he disappeared for good?*

I round the hall and stop dead in my tracks. Coming towards me are Alec and Marya. Normally I wouldn't bat an eye at seeing them together, but if my eyes aren't deceiving me today, they're holding hands! I swallow the lump that's formed in my throat. I try to move, to turn around, something, but find my feet firmly planted to the ground and my eyes fixed on the two of them. *When did this happen?*

I watch the two of them together, seemingly unaware of my presence. Alec tells her a joke and she laughs, throwing back her strawberry-blonde hair. She nestles her cheek on his shoulder and gives his hand a squeeze.

Across the hall, Alec's eyes finally lock onto mine. Like a deer caught in the headlights, he stops mid-stride and drops Marya's hand. I purse my lips, wanting to look away but can't. It's not like he's doing anything wrong. We aren't together or anything. But there's still a small amount of jealousy that's bubbled up from deep inside that I guess I didn't know was there.

Alec turns towards Marya and whispers something in her ear. She nods her head and begins walking ahead of him, towards the mess hall no doubt. As she passes me, she gives me a small, meek smile and I'm not sure what to make of it.

I return my eyes to Alec, who has narrowed down the distance between us. His hands fidget nervously at his sides. I watch as he plasters a smile on his face and greets me. "Hey there, Willow. Good morning."

I guess it's a two greeting kind of morning. I nod my head, not sure what to say. Awkwardness creeps up and fills the space between us.

"You wanna go for a walk?" he finally says, breaking the tension.

I let out the breath I'd been holding and say, "Sure."
He puts his hand on his hip, creating a triangle
with his arm. When he did this in the past, I always placed
my arm through his, now I'm not sure what to do.

"As friends," he insinuates.

A small flood of relief pours through me. "As
friends," I repeat, reminding myself this is what I had
originally wanted. Now that Alec wasn't vying for my
attention anymore, things seem weird and distant. Darn it,
I liked being the center of his universe! *Did I?* How selfish
is that?

I place my arm in his and we walk outside, taking
in the crisp air. The warm colors of autumn surround us.
After a few minutes, Alec breaks the silence. "Getting chilly
out here," he says as he rocks back on his feet. "Are you
okay? Do you need a jacket?"

I smile at him. He's still the same Alec. Always
making sure I'm okay.

"No, I'm good. You're keeping me warm." He gives
my hand a small tap with his. "So, you and Marya," I say,
cringing that I brought it up. I can't for the life of me figure
out why I'm so dang jealous! But I may as well talk about
the elephant in the room.

I watch as Alec clears his throat. The breeze rustles
his hair, making him look strikingly beautiful. "Marya's a
very special girl," he says, lost in thought. I watch his face
as he talks about Marya and I can feel his happiness. He
returns his attention to me.

"In some ways she reminds me of you. She's smart

and kind. She never says a bad word about anyone. I guess you could say things are beginning to step away from the friendship realm, if that's what you're asking. Nothing's official yet, of course. I did want to talk to you first."

I bite my lip, not sure what to say. I'm happy for both of them, really, it's just, deep down, there's an unsettled feeling and I'm not sure what to make of it. Is it because I miss Tony? Is it because I'm jealous of Marya and Alec or both? I want Alec to be happy and I want Marya to be happy as well. It's in this moment that I realize I haven't officially let go of Alec. I said it aloud, and I said it with my actions with Tony, but I never said it with my heart. "Are you happy?" I ask him. Because if he is, who am I to hold him back? That would be selfish of me and that's not a character trait I want to possess. I watch a smile light his face.

"To be honest, yeah, I'm happy. It took a while but I think things are finally looking up again."

I cringe inside and let my eyes drop. I want to be happy for him, I really do! I just can't find it in myself. So I resolve to pretend to be happy for him. It's the least I can do.

"Well, Alec, if you're happy, then I'm happy. Go get your girl," I say playfully.

He laughs that laugh of his that I have always enjoyed and it sets me at ease. The man I once loved, and probably always will, is happy. Who am I to take that away from him?

He gives my hand a pat. "Can I walk you to the

mess hall?" he asks.

I think for a moment but shake my head. "No, I'm good. I'm going to take a walk first." He gives me one of his million-dollar smiles.

"Don't stay out too long." We part ways and I watch him walk back inside.

I take a deep breath and walk into the woods. I walk farther and farther in until I can no longer see the camp. Eventually, I find a large oak tree to sit beneath. Its leaves have almost all fallen off and I can see the overcast sky through the bare branches. I lean my head back and listen to the sounds of nature.

"*Where are you, Tony?*" A single tear rolls down my cheek. I miss him so much it hurts. I pull my legs up to my chest and squeeze, making sure I'm tethered to the ground. I let my mind wander with memories of Tony and me at the lake house. I remember how comfortable he felt hunting and gathering our dinner. How he played his guitar so smoothly and beautifully. How he held me in the dead of night after I lost my mother. Never once pressuring me to do anything I didn't want to do. Always being the respectful gentlemen he is.

"*Willow?*" I hear my name so softly it's as if it's carried by the wind. I think it might be a figment of my imagination until I hear it a second time...then a third.

I look around me, "Who's there?" I ask aloud. The leaves on the ground and the few left in the trees rustle in the wind. I look in all directions but I don't see anyone.

"*Willow, it's me. Tony.*"

My heart skips a beat at the sound of his name. Can this be real? I jump to my feet and look all around, desperate to see him. *"Can I see you?"* I ask him. I'm not completely sure that I haven't conjured his voice up with my imagination, but still, I hope. I wait for a while with no response.

I realize that my mind is playing tricks on me but then I hear him come through my thoughts again. *"I'm near, but I don't want to accidently hurt you. Zack is very unpredictable and can take control at any moment; I don't want you to be in the way when he does."*

"I want to see you," I reiterate, placing urgency in my tone. I want to see that he's still alive. That he's still fighting for me. *"Please, Tony. Just for a moment."* I wait with bated breath. I wait with all hope that he will come through these trees...that I can see his beautiful face. I wait and search for him, biting my lip in anticipation. The consequences don't even cross my mind. It's as if I've put blinders on and can't see the bad that could come from this.

Right when I think I can't wait anymore, I see him step out from the trees. My heart beats heavily inside my chest at the sight of him. Can this be a mirage or some type of fantasy that I've conjured up? I know the mind can be a very powerful thing. I want to run to him and jump in his arms. I want to kiss him with all that I'm worth and feel his comforting embrace encompass me. I lose myself in my thoughts and before I know it, my legs are moving faster than my mind. I cover the distance between us and run into his arms. *He's really here*, I think as I crash into him.

He catches me and pulls me close to him. "*We can't be doing this, Willow. It's too dangerous,*" he tells me, his lips kissing my hair.

"*One minute Tony...just give me one minute,*" I beg.

I feel his posture relax an infinitesimal amount, but it's enough to know that he'll give me this minute.

"I love you," I say to him aloud.

He places his hand in my hair and pulls my head back. "I love you too," he says back to me and immediately places his lips on mine. It's a kiss like no other. The kind where your toes curl and every nerve ending in your body is heightened. I run my hands through his hair, never wanting it to end. He places his hand on my cheek and releases me.

"I have to go, Willow. I don't want to, but I have to. It's not safe for me to be so close to you. Your life means more to me than anything and I can't put it in the hands of Zack." His yellow eyes are filled with love and fierce concern.

I nod my head, understanding what he's saying. He wouldn't be able to live with himself if he hurt me...even if it's not really him doing it. I lift up on my toes for one last kiss, never believing that it could be our last. I don't open my eyes even though I can sense that he's gone. Instead, I imagine that he's still right here with me. Still running his hands through my hair and telling me that everything's going to be okay.

"*I'll never leave you, Willow,*" I hear him say softly in my mind.

"*And for that I'm grateful,*" I say in response. I open my eyes and his absence is more than apparent. I feel so naked and vulnerable standing out here in the forest alone. With Tony around, I feel invincible and powerful, like nothing could harm me. I sigh from his absence. "*I miss you,*" I tell him, not sure if he can still hear me.

Several seconds go by before I hear a response. "*I miss you too. More than you'll ever know.*"

I sit back down on the soft, forest floor and curl my knees up to my chest. Leaning my head against the tree trunk, I close my eyes. If I imagine hard enough, I can still feel him with me; not standing at a safe distance, but right next to me. But, knowing that he's okay and that he's near is more than I could have asked for. A leaf falls on my lap. I open my eyes and stare at the intricate lines drawn into it by nature.

"*Stay with me a while?*" I ask, hoping he agrees.

"*Of course. Willow, even when Zack forces me to leave, the second I come back to myself I go in search of you. You give me something to live for, something to fight for. When you feel like you're alone, just know that I'm not far off. That I'm going to always come back to you, no matter how long it takes.*"

I inwardly sigh at his words. So poetic that it makes my heart soar. "*Is that what you tell all the girls?*" I ask, trying to lighten the mood.

I can feel him laughing in my mind. Closing my eyes, I imagine his smile. I hear a rustle in the bushes and open them. A single rose lay in front of me, the thorns having been picked off. I smile, take the rose in my hand,

and rub the velvety petals in between my fingers. "*It's beautiful,*" I say. "*Thank you.*"

I hear a faint, "*I love you,*" in my head before I feel Tony's presence disappear altogether. It's as if he's hollowed out a space in my head and heart that only he can occupy. I sigh and place the rose against my nose, relishing the sweet smell.

I hear another rustling in the bushes like before. I smile, thinking it's Tony, and stand up. "Should I close my eyes again?" I ask aloud, wondering if he has another flower or some other random something from the woods. Or maybe he decided against leaving me.

I don't hear a response, just a footstep, then two, approaching. Startled, I look behind me and nearly choke on my next breath. Three men stand just a few feet from me… The man in the lead stares at me with cold, hard, red eyes. Reaper!

Backing up, I wildly look around for a way out. I can't think or breathe. All I can do is wait, paralyzed by fear and shock. Then, as if hit by a brick, all my training comes barreling back into my mind. All the things Tony taught me, and more that I learned on my own, kick in. I scurry back to put some more distance between these three men and me, but as soon as I do, I bump into another tree. I try to side step the tree but two of the men come around to my sides, blocking me in. Terror runs through my veins now that I realize I'm cornered.

"Tony," I whisper desperately. I can't believe I allowed myself to get into this mess. I should never have left the camp.

"You shouldn't be out here all alone, sugar," says the man with red eyes who has taken the lead. My heart crystalizes, frozen in fear when I hear Zack's pet name for me come from this man's lips. This isn't a Reaper; it's one of Zack's men. He's controlling him!

My eyes dart all around me, looking for an escape route even though there isn't one. Panicked, I start pulling up the large Oak tree behind the three men.

The man being controlled by Zack clucks his tongue at me. "Willow, Willow, Willow. When will you ever learn? I know all the tricks in your book. You can't fool me anymore. I have you right where I need you and now you're coming with me." Zack's trademark smile etches across this nameless man's face, which creeps me out even more!

"You will NEVER take me alive!" I spit vehemently at him. I focus my powers and step backwards, straight through the tree behind me. I do it so fast that I barely notice the lead guy's eyes change color or the disoriented look cross over his features. I turn to run only to be scooped into someone's arms. The smell of earth and soap tickles my senses before I feel the needle being shoved into my neck. I wince as I try to get away, but a dizzying sensation immediately overtakes me. The world begins spinning out of control. My knees weaken and I'm scooped back up into his arms. I look up to see Tony staring down at me. I want to reach my hand up to touch his cheek but he looks completely distorted…and has red eyes…and…my world goes black.

Cold and shaking, I wake up.

My hands are bound behind my back and my cheek is on a cold, concrete floor. I've been gagged and my mouth feels dry like sandpaper. I try to run my tongue around it but the gag keeps me from doing much. When I open my eyes, I find that a blindfold prevents me from seeing.

I concentrate on Connor's gift, trying to wiggle out of the chains that bind me, but to no avail. *What is happening to me?* I shake my arms again and feel the IV that is stuck into my arm.

"Well, well, well. Look who's finally awake," a strangely familiar voice calls to me.

I try to speak, but my words come out muffled. My head is still swimming from the drug I was given earlier.

"There are some people here who've been *dying* to meet you."

I try to use my strength to break the binding on my arms but it doesn't work. I grit my teeth against the gag giving up, realizing my powers have been stripped from me. The cold blade of a knife touches the side of my cheek. I wince but don't move. The knife moves up my cheek and

I shiver in fright. My heart starts racing; any second this person could end my life. The knife catches underneath the fabric that binds my eyes and rips it clean apart.

The brightness of the room floods into my eyes, making them burn. I wince at the sudden change and recoil back into myself. "Now, be a good girl and everything will work out okay."

I catch my first, blurry glimpse of the person standing before me. He looks vaguely familiar but I can't place him. He's older than the men in the woods, probably pushing his upper forties or so. He comes closer to me and I can see the myriad of colors he possesses in his eyes. I catch a glimpse of red, neon yellow, blue, purple, and brown.

I take in a sharp breath. How did he manage this?

He lets off an evil laugh. "What, do you think you're the only special one out there?"

Blinking a few times, I try to get my eyes to adjust. I mumble through the gag but it does no good.

He leans in and brings the knife to my face again. My heart stops and I close my eyes. A frustrated tear falls down my cheek. He slowly cuts one side of the gag. I feel him pull it out of my mouth before I open my eyes again.

"You don't recognize me, do you?" His face is only inches from mine. I can smell a hint of alcohol on his breath and it makes me want to gag.

I blink a few times as my eyes begin to focus better. My heart starts racing as the realization sets in. "Mr. Blake," I say with my hoarse voice. *Alec's dad!*

He smiles and stands up. "How's my boy doing?"

I stare at him in horror, but I don't answer his question. "Why are you doing this?"

He raises an eyebrow at me. Ignoring the question, he instead changes the IV bag. He pulls out a syringe filled with an opaque liquid. He flicks it with his finger, making sure the bubbles float to the top. I gulp as he slowly injects it directly into my IV.

A warming sensation runs through my veins. "What was that?" I ask, my voice sounding strange, foreign.

"Just a little something to help you with your powers. Don't you worry; you won't have enough control of your abilities to do any damage or escape, but just enough to be able to show them off a little." He steps on the pedal of the stainless-steel trash bin to open the lid. Chucking the needle and the empty IV bag inside it, he lets the lid fall with a heavy thud.

My stomach is filled with knots as I think about Alec. What would this do to him? Does he know his dad's a psycho?

"I'm hardly crazy, Willow." He laughs.

I notice his eye color is focused more on the dark green aspect of his gift. My brain starts clearing a little more as whatever he gave me clears the other drugs from my system. "Hasn't anyone told you yet that it's an invasion of privacy to read minds or that it's plain old rude?" I ask, annoyed.

He looks at me with an arched brow. "Ha! Do you think I care about being rude to a lab rat?" He rolls his eyes when I glare at him. "Anyhow, you are merely a variable in a wide-range experiment."

"What are you talking about, Blake?" I spit at him.

He looks unaffected by my tone or my informal use of his name. "I am saying that you aren't nearly as special as you think you are." He points his finger towards his eyes. "It's obvious that you aren't the only one with multiple abilities. Our only question is how *you* managed to acquire yours. I checked your charts and you weren't given anything special other than an immunization that would allow you to read minds."

The wheels in my brain start churning as he speaks. Why would it still matter to him how I got my gift if they already know how to replicate it? I see his eyes turning a deeper shade of green. He's trying to dig around in my thoughts! "Figure it out yourself," I tell him as I throw my shield up. I don't know if it worked because none of my abilities worked earlier, but I cross my fingers.

A look of outrage scrunches his reddened face. "How dare you, you little twit!" He grabs my shoulders and starts shaking me.

I feel the IV loosen from all of the jostling. I try to rip my arms free but the constraints are too tight. I don't have enough strength to use more than one gift at a time.

"You think I can't see your silver eyes? You aren't even supposed to have that gift!" He gives me a look of indignation.

Not sure what he means by that statement, I focus on hearing his thoughts. It's hard because I have to keep my shield up at the same time. Sweat accumulates on my brow as I try to focus on the little power that these drugs are letting through. Finally, I hear, "*We didn't even create such an immunization. It must have mutated from something else. why can't I do it? He said I'd get all of her gifts!* "He looks at my eyes. "What the?" He slaps me in the face.

The searing heat snaps me out of his mind and sends tears to my eyes. I stretch my jaw, happy it's not broken, as I stare up at him.

"I said don't hurt her!" Tony calls with an angry voice. My eyes find Tony walking furiously towards Mr. Blake. Tony's eyes are crimson red as he grabs the front of Blake's shirt. He pulls him to where he's only inches from his face. "You idiot!"

Blake cringes as Tony roars at him. "She tried to play me! Look at her eyes; she's trying to read my thoughts!" He points his finger at me in a jabbing motion.

I lie there staring in stunned silence at Tony going head to head with my kidnapper. *Except he's not your Tony, Willow, his eyes are red.*

Looking from me to Blake, he yells a final order. "Go get the connection started." He lets go of his shirt collar.

Blake doesn't waste a moment before he hurriedly exits the room. When did Tony become in charge?

Tony comes to my side. The first thing he does is adjusts the connection on my IV. I instantly begin feeling what little powers I had control of lessen.

Then he kneels down on the floor, moves closer to me, and examines my reddened cheek. He seems angry or is it concern that I see etched in his expression? He reaches his fingertips to the whelp on my face. I close my eyes and pray that Tony has found a way to get out of Zack's control. That he will remove my bindings, take out that needle, and swoop me to safety.

Opening my eyes, I find Tony gone. I look around the room for him but he's not there. Tears spring to my eyes. I have no idea what in the world is happening. Then, just as quickly as he left, he appears again with something white in his hand.

He strides over to me, sits back down next to me, places the ice pack on my cheek, and says, "That wasn't supposed to happen."

I lean my cheek into his hand and stare at him with hopeful eyes.

Then he grins and my stomach clenches. "You think I care that the idiot slapped you, don't you, sugar?" He pushes my hair back behind my ears in such a contrastingly affectionate manner that makes no sense when coupled with his horrible words. "No, what I care about is that you are worth a lot of money to me and he messed up your pretty little face right before I can introduce you to the bidders."

My mind doesn't wrap around what he's saying. "Bidders?" I ask. All hope for Tony overcoming Zack's control is lost in this moment.

"Yes, bidders. Your blood is worth a lot of money, sugar. Just look what it did for old man Blake. I can market your powers with endless possibilities. Best part is, they will have to keep coming back to get the goods. I told my dad that I wanted power and, sure enough, I will be the most powerful man in the world because of you." He smiles proudly.

Seeing that look on Tony sickens me even more. "So you are going to sell my blood?" I ask directly.

"Yes," he says bluntly.

"Why aren't you here, Zack? You finally got me! So stop using Tony to do your dirty work and show yourself. Only a coward would do what you're doing," I yell.

"I would if I were nearby, but I have a few business transactions to complete first. I had no idea our Tony would have actually led me to you so easily. He did so well at staying away from you for weeks. I started thinking that I'd have to find another way to entice you to turn yourself in. Turns out all I had to do was let him be himself for a bit and have my men follow him," he says.

My blood turns to ice as I think of my dad, Sabby, and all of the other people that I love. He has so many pawns that he could easily use against me.

He leans in closer to me, his familiar face only inches from mine. My pulse quickens. "You really do love me, don't you?" he whispers.

I shake my head. "I don't love you, Zack. I love Tony. Now let him go!"

He gives me a half smile. "I'm not stupid enough to throw down all of my cards when the game is getting so good, sugar." He puts his hand behind the back of my neck and pulls my head up off the concrete floor, to where only an inch separates us. He looks at me with a twisted expression that doesn't belong to my Tony, and then he presses his lips to mine. His lips may belong to Tony, but this kiss isn't his. As I struggle to move my head out of his grip, he pushes me tighter against him, crushing my lips further into his. All thoughts of Tony kissing me are completely out the window. This is Zack, and knowing that his lips are on mine, that he is experiencing this kiss, makes me want to puke. I try to struggle to get my hands free but once again, I have no luck. Thankfully, he releases me and my head thumps back on the hard ground, which sends stars sprawling across my vision.

I spit at him but he moves quickly out of the away, avoiding my insult. "Don't ever do that again!" I hate that there are tears in my eyes when I say it but I can't help it. My stomach rolls with nausea as I think of that sick, twisted kiss.

He just laughs. "I'll send the guys in to get you in a few, sugar. Please try to use some of that healing power to get rid of that bruise on your pretty little face."

"I wish I had the power to forget everything you just did!" I yell.

He flippantly tosses a coin in the air, catching it, he places it in his pocket. He laughs as he walks out of the room.

I sit up in the darkened room, my mind wandering, not being able to connect the dots. My blood is about to be sold on the black market, to the highest bidders... Then what? Am I going to be kept prisoner forever just so my blood can be dripped slowly from my veins? I lean my head, the only extremity I'm able to control, against the wall.

I scream in frustration and toss my head from side to side. It's the only thing I can think to do in a time like this. I hear the door open and a light shines in the room.

Old man Blake sticks his head in and shows me a large syringe. Waving it at me, he says, "If you can't keep quiet, I can make you. Gives you something to think about, huh?"

I quiet down at his threats. He closes the door and I'm flooded back into darkness.

I slouch against the wall and allow the time to pass. Every now and again, someone comes in and injects another dose of the medicine into my IV. I allow myself to shut down because if I think, I hurt. I lie in the darkness, waiting for the bidding.

Time passes, how long I'm not sure. I feel a foot jabbing my ribs and wake immediately. I sit up awkwardly and look up at the person in the room. Blake and Tony stand before me. They each grab a hold under my arms and hoist me to my feet. Since I'm still bound, it makes it near impossible to stand on my own. They drag me over to a wheelchair and stuff me in it. My hands get rebound onto the chair itself, making escape of any sort an impossibility, at least while my powers remain dulled.

I'm wheeled down a long empty hall. There are doors on either side intermittently, but they remain closed. From the level I sit on, I can't see inside the small, glass windows on top of the doors. My mind wanders as I'm pushed along. I wonder who knows I'm here. Have my friends started looking for me?

We turn down yet another hallway and come to a random red door. Although I'm sure it's not random in their eyes. Tony opens the door and Blake wheels me inside. I can feel Tony staring holes into the back of my head. I don't turn around and look in his direction. I can't hide my feelings right now and I don't want Zack to get his kicks from the betrayal that I'm feeling.

Instead, I focus in on the cameras that are dispersed around the room, each of them angled towards the center of the area. A large mirror covers an entire wall. I'm wheeled into the center of the room and turned to face the mirror. The brakes are applied on the wheelchair and I'm locked in place. My mind feels fuzzy and numb from all of the injections I've received.

Tony catches my eye in the mirror behind me. I gasp when I see his eyes. The red is giving way to a strange combination of twists and curls of neon yellow. A stark realization is starting to peak in his expression. Two large men come into the room instantly, grabbing a hold of Tony. I see him struggle with them for a moment in the doorway before his eyes turn red again. Then he shrugs them off and straightens out his shirt before he exits the room, leaving Blake and me alone.

Blake turns away from the mirror and looks straight at me. "No funny business or I'll make sure that Tony never sees the light of day again. Understood?"

I nod my head, not wanting anything to happen to

Tony. I can't help but wonder what just happened though. Is Tony starting to break through? Did Zack momentarily lose control?

A fake smile overtakes Blake's face as he turns towards the mirror. I can't help but look at myself. My face is haunted and pale. My eyes have dark shadows underneath them and the colors in my irises look dulled, like how colors get faded by the sun. My hair is literally all over the place as if someone teased it and then left it to its own devices. I don't really care what I look like though, I'll be lucky enough to make it out of this nightmare alive.

Blake presses a blue button on the side of the glass and a room full of people appears where my reflection once was.

Two-way glass, I should have known.

He walks around the room, methodically turning on each camera. My stomach sinks more and more with every red light that appears below each one. My mouth goes dry at the thought of who is watching me. How many people are in on this evil plot to purchase my blood? Looking towards the room on the other side of the glass, I notice at least ten people are seated inside. How many more are on the other side of those cameras?

"We're live," he says to me before leaving the room. I hear the click of the door that seals my fate.

A tall man with balding, grey hair and a long, pointy nose approaches on his side of the glass. He pushes a button, activating an intercom system. "Good afternoon, Willow, my name is Mr. Gables. I'm the director of one of the compounds in the south. From what we've heard about your abilities, well, you've become quite the talk."

I wonder why he would tell me his name and his position. My stomach churns as I contemplate the fact that he obviously doesn't foresee me ever getting out of this imprisonment. Nods of approval emanate from the remaining people behind the glass. I swallow hard. Like vampires, these people will be bleeding me dry before long. The thought makes me nauseous. I try to squirm in my chair but I'm unable to move more than a fraction of an inch.

He releases the button and turns to speak to a man behind him. I can't hear what they're saying. All I see are nodding heads and lips moving. They talk for a moment and then he turns back to me. The static over the intercom tells me he's about to say something again. "We've been told that you've been given an injection that limits your abilities for safety purposes. Can you show us anything you can do while still on the medication?"

I scoff at him. Is he serious? Does he honestly believe that I'm just going to sell my soul to the highest bidder? I laugh under my breath. He lets go of the button again and turns back around to the same man. I can see the irritation in his stature, his face reddening. The man behind him puts his two hands up, trying to appease the other man. I can see him apologizing profusely before he scurries out of the room. I ignore them and stare down at my knees like they are the most interesting thing in the world. I refuse to look up at these sorry excuses for human beings.

A few minutes later, the lock clicks on my door and in walks Blake. His face is red and contorted with rage. "We should have known you were going to try and make a fool out of us," he says angrily under his breath. He turns and smiles towards the people on the other side of the glass, then turns back towards me, a frown hardening on his face.

I look away from him and try to ignore the shuffling of feet headed in my direction. I wonder if Blake is going to slap me again. Then I hear a grunt as someone is thrown at my feet. I see his copper hair first. "Tony," I say breathlessly. His hands are bound and he looks badly beaten. His eye and jaw are black and blue. Dried blood cakes the side of his face. I choke a sob. I try to get my arms free so I can help him, but the bindings won't budge.

Blake drags Tony to his feet. "The next time your boy won't just be roughed up. Since we don't need him to hunt you down anymore, there's no reason to keep him alive. You get what I mean?" He opens the side of his white lab coat so I can see the shiny revolver he has in a holster. "So, I'd suggest you make nice and do what these people ask. Mmm-K?"

I look down at Tony, whose breathing is labored, his arm bent at an unnatural angle. "His bone is broken!" I yell, my stomach twisting in knots. I look up at the people behind the glass. Nobody seems concerned at all to see Tony in such a state. How can they be so heartless?

Blake laughs. "Well, he tried to fight back and you know Tony. He's strong, so we couldn't really take it easy on him, now could we?" He checks his watch, tapping on the glass.

I glare at him. The fact that this jerk face has to end everything in a question makes me want to smack him in the face with a fireball. Why can't I have that gift?

He looks back up from his watch, letting me know how much time I am causing him to waste. "Are you going to play nice?" He smiles, realizing that he hit the sweet spot by threatening the man I love.

I grit my teeth. "Yes." He smiles triumphantly and begins dragging Tony out of the room. "Stop!" I yell.

He stops and looks at me with feigned annoyance.

"You want me to show them my powers? Then bring Tony here; I want to heal him. But you will have to free up at least one of my hands," I demand.

He opens his mouth ready to say no, but then looks to the people behind the mirror and back at me. His lips spread out in an unnatural grin and I can see his sense of reasoning go out the door with the promise of large sums of money. "Fine. But you better not try anything. You don't want us to mess him up even more, do you?" he asks, giving me one last threat of what'll happen to Tony if I choose to act out.

I take a deep breath to avoid telling off this jerk. I want to punch that stupid, fake grin off his face but instead I say, "Yes. I'm just going to heal him."

"Assistance!" Blake snaps to some goons who I hadn't noticed standing at the doorway. They step in and pick Tony up under the arms.

Tony groans, still unconscious, as he's dragged across the room. Blake loosens the binding around my left hand and gives me the evil eye when I'm able to finally pull my hand free. "Watch your step, Mmm-K?" he says.

I roll my eyes dramatically and stretch my hand out towards Tony, but I can't reach him. The men drag Tony closer and drop him at my feet like a sack of potatoes. Since that was the end of their assistance, I have to reach down and use my fingertips to grab the fabric of his sleeve. Using one hand is hard! Especially since they released my non-dominant, left hand. I pull on his shirtsleeve and bring his arm to where it's sitting limp on my lap. I examine the broken bone, his arm bent at an unnatural angle. Placing my hand gingerly over it and close my eyes, I focus on calling my powers. It feels like I'm intoxicated as I reach through my fuzzy mind to focus on healing. I concentrate and push myself through the hazy fog of medication, trying to fix him. After a few minutes of exerting all of my mental power, I feel the sweat dripping off my brow.

The sound of Tony taking in a loud breath makes me open my eyes. "Willow?"

I gasp. My Tony is here with me. Not Zack. I stare into his beautiful, yellow eyes. His face contorts with horror as he realizes where we are. Then the anger takes over and he moves to stand up, but the pain has him doubling over. I fixed a bone but not the other internal damage. I have no idea the complete extent of his injuries.

Blake starts a slow clap. "Bravo!" He nods to his men. Understanding the signal, they come and subdue

Tony so he can't try anything. Then Blake looks at the people behind the glass and says with a raised voice, "You see, if she had full control of her powers, she'd be able to heal him completely. However, as you just saw, she did a wonderful job of healing his broken wrist." He clucks at the men and they bring Tony closer to the glass, forcing him to hold out his wrist to them for inspection. He forces him to move his wrist in a circular motion to prove it's healed.

Several people push up against the window to get a better look. Then I watch in disgust as they begin smiling and clapping. Who are these sick people?

An older woman with ginger hair and a shrewd expression, steps up to the intercom. "We see that her gift is quite impressive and would love to see her full powers outside of sedation sometime. But, I still fail to see how her blood will allow us to possess her same gifts."

Blake walks closer to the glass and points to his eyes. "If you can see my eyes, you will notice that I have several different colors present in my irises. Each of these colors represents a different ability. I gained this yesterday, when I was injected with a very small amount of Ms. Mosby's blood. To better show you my gift, I will finish healing this man so he can tell you more about the process."

The people behind the glass watch him with perplexed expressions. Blake puts his hand on Tony's shoulder and I watch as his eyes turn a deep, navy blue. Eventually, Tony goes from doubled over to standing up without help. Blake removes his hand and looks at the people who are clapping again in complete bewilderment.

Tony turns to look at me. His lips spread apart in that Cheshire grin. His eyes are beet red.

My stomach flips upside down as I realize that Zack only left Tony while he was being beaten. What a coward!

Tony turns to address the crowd. He takes a bow first. "My name is Zack Hastings, son of Dr. Hastings. After my late father and I extensively researched the reasons behind Ms. Mosby's multiple abilities, we found that her blood held the key to recreating her powers. At first, we spent time trying to configure what mixtures of inoculations caused this, but that research came back inconclusive. We only confirmed the fact that Ms. Mosby is obviously a very special girl." He dramatically waves his hand towards me.

I send mind bullets his way, but they have no effect. If only I had that ability too.

He continues. "After much deliberation, we decided to test out injecting a small amount of the sample into my bloodstream. This was the ultimate key to replicating her powers. So, we are here today because I am willing to share this new ability with you. For a price, that is."

Mr. Gables walks up to the intercom again. "I met Dr. Hastings's son, Zack, a few years ago. I don't know who you are trying to fool, but you are *not* Zack Hastings."

"Touché! I was wondering if you would take notice. I remember meeting you too, Mr. Gables. How is that granddaughter of yours doing? April was her name?" Tony smiles as the man lets off a bewildered expression. Tony answers his unasked question. "I am controlling this man that you see before you. Circumstances prevented me from attending this conference in physical person, but I am mentally here."

The entire crowd gawks at him, stunned. Mr. Gables presses the intercom again and asks, "How are you controlling this man?"

"I'm not ready to divulge that secret just yet." When they look outraged, he adds, "Don't worry, one great thing at a time. Trust me; you all will be the first people I'll call when I'm ready to market this particular shot." Tony, I mean Zack, doesn't wait for them to calm down. He finalizes the conversation by lifting his hands. "Let the bidding begin."

The people behind the glass pull out their tablets and begin furiously typing on them. I assume there is some sort of electronic bidding process that they are partaking in. Every once in a while, one of them will look at me and seem to make a decision, then they type some more on their tablets.

Blake presses the button on the glass, turning it back into a mirror. Then he leaves the room with his goons in tow.

Tony, who has focused on his tablet, turns to exit a moment later. He stops and smiles at me with an air of superiority before he exits the room melodramatically and with flair. The lock clicks in place, leaving me alone with my thoughts.

Something breaks inside me. My breathing is completely unnatural, coated with fear. Tears blur my vision as I try to hold it together. I'm going to be bled dry for these people. How can anyone allow this to happen? I'm not sure how much more I can take. How can those people see me in my shackles and not care that I'm being held prisoner? Can't they see that I am still a human being?

Something tickles at my memory. That's when I look down. In the heat of the situation and the excitement for the money to be made, they forgot to secure my left hand. I can't see the people on the other side of the mirror. In fact, they could have left for all I know, but I can't be sure that they won't be witness to what I'm about to do. Careful not to draw attention to myself, I slowly move my hand up to my right arm and pull the IV needle out of my vein. Blood pools in a small dot on my hand. Then I start working on the constraints.

My heart is pounding because I have no idea how long I have. I don't know if someone has seen what I'm doing and notified Zack's minions. I bend down and unshackle my feet. Thankfully, they were only bound with tight leather straps and not with cuffs that require a key. Once I'm free, I put my hands back on top of the chair and sit still. I try to pretend that nothing out of the norm is happening in case anybody noticed my earlier movements.

I close my eyes and focus on clearing my mind. *How long will those drugs last?* I try to push my hand through the arm of the chair but I can't move it far. I find too much resistance. Frustrated that I'm not magically able to kick all of the drugs out of my system in an instant, I shake my head.

My heart is still beating too quickly. I take long,

deep breaths and instead of focusing on moving through objects, I focus on healing. I breathe in and out as I try to heal myself. My thoughts start becoming crisper and my vision less blurry. I try again to push my hand through the arm of the chair and it goes straight through.

The lock on the door jiggles. Without further thought, I jump out of the chair and run to the wall. I push my arm through as well as one leg. The door starts opening and, before I can see who is coming in, I jump through the wall.

I fall to my knees in the middle of a long corridor of more offices. I decide my best bet is to keep moving in the same direction. Eventually, I will make it to an exterior wall. I step through another wall and land in a large, empty office. I don't bother with going around the desk. I walk straight through it and out another wall. I look around and find myself in a bathroom. By the nasty smell wafting off the urinals, I realize it's a men's bathroom, *ick!* I see a set of feet moving under a stall. A toilet flushes.

I run through another wall before they can see me and I'm falling! A second later, I hit the ground with a thud. The air is knocked from my lungs. It takes several seconds before I'm finally able to take in a breath of the frosty night air.

The sound of an alarm going off inside of the building gives me the push to get moving again. I stand up and run.

EIGHT

Run! I exhale puffs of smoke as my labored breath meets the icy air.

I wasn't awake when they took me here, so I have no earthly idea where I am. From what I can see, I'm in an urbanized industrial area. I run through an abandoned parking lot towards an outcropping of buildings.

I don't hear any pursuers yet, but the alarms haven't quieted in the distance. Wispy clouds stream across the full moon, giving a creepy feel to the night. I imagine the sound of helicopters and vehicles will be roaring to life soon. I'm their moneymaker. There is no way they are going to let me go without a fight.

I reach the first building before I hear any sign of pursuit. I turn around and see him running for me. *Tony!* Even though my heart wishes he were coming to save me, I don't dare turn to him. I know Zack well enough to realize that there is no way he will relinquish control over him at a time like this.

I push aside the hopeless idea that Tony found a way to break free of Zack's power and is coming to save me. This isn't a fairy tale. I have to save myself.

He's gaining on me, so I push myself harder. I whiz down streets of tall, empty buildings that cast eerie shadows across the ground. The night is dark but the moon is bright enough that I can't find easy cover.

I take a fast right, hoping to lose him. I run behind an alley that lines a steel graveyard of refineries and more old buildings. Something about this place is frighteningly familiar. The sound of his feet hitting the pavement behind me propels me forward. My eyes must be glowing neon yellow with how hard I'm pushing this ability.

"Don't worry, Willow! I'm not going to hurt you." His breath doesn't even sound winded. I don't dare glance behind me again, not even when he adds an evil, "much," to the end of that sentence a second later.

My stomach drops with his words. *The vision!* I remember it as I spot a fork in the road a few yards ahead. I don't debate whether I should take it or stay on this straight path. I remember the vision. The fork leads to a dead end. I fake like I'm going to go left but I keep going straight. I push the limits of my power, running so ridiculously fast that I can only imagine there's a smoke trail beneath my sneakers.

I can see water up ahead. The moon reflects off its shiny surface. Soon, I find myself at the end of a street with another choice to be made. Left or right. I don't have time to really study the different routes because he's so close now. *Right!* I decide at the very last second. I turn and find myself running along a street lined with boarded-up shops and restaurants.

My heart is like a jackhammer pounding in my chest. The sound of his pounding feet hitting the pavement is so close now. He's had this ability longer than I have and sure knows how to push it further. I'm sure the fact that he hasn't been drugged helps.

I'm shoved from behind, sending me plummeting to the concrete. Reaching my hands out just in time, I keep my face from smashing into the ground. I wince at the stinging sensation as I feel the cold ground scraping the skin from my knees and palms.

He laughs, only inches behind me. Like in the vision, it's just Tony and me. Nobody else around and once again, he has me in his snares. I think about how I should have killed Zack when I had the chance! If only I had sent ten buildings tumbling on top of that creep instead of just one.

I stand up and turn around slowly, with my head faced towards the ground. I don't know if my heart can take seeing the image of the man I love, looking so smugly at me. I know what I have to do, but will I be able to do it once I see him?

I can feel Tony only a breath's distance apart. He doesn't say anything. Instead, he lifts my chin with his finger and forces me to look at him. My heart betrays me by perking up at the sight of him. So many emotions run through me and no words can express the way I feel. Something incomprehensible tells me that even if he hunts me for the rest of my life, I will not hate him. His copper hair shines under the moonlight and his eyes glow an eerie, burgundy red. I hate the evil in those eyes. Not an internal evil, but one that has been forced upon him. If only I could hate him. It would make this easier.

I don't mean for my plea to come out in a throaty whisper, one that begs him to see me, but it does. I need him to see through everything that has been done to him, to us, and to break away from the puppet master who pulls his strings. It comes out as I plead, "Please, Tony." I hope beyond hope that the simple words will stop what is sure to come next.

He doesn't so much as flinch at my plea. He smirks. "You have been a giant pain, sugar! I will have to punish you for this attempt at escaping. Although I will say that the bounty on your little head just got a little higher, so thanks for that." He grabs my shoulder and squeezes.

My blood boils and the exasperation of the situation overtakes me. I can't stop what happens next, even though I want so badly to. The edges of my vision blur with a bloody-red haze. My heart beats ferociously as I look into his eyes. His look turns from pure confidence, to doubt. Then fear.

I hate Zack for doing this to me! I hate his dad for cursing me with these gifts that people will hunt me for. I hate that Tony has been taken over and that there will be no way for me to save him now. That there is no out! My body is shaking with rage when he turns to run.

This time *I* chase him down the long boardwalk that lines the lake. He thinks he's fast, but my hatred pushes me faster. He doesn't make it further than a few yards before

I jump on him and he goes crashing to the ground. He tries to fight against me but I use my strength to hold him down. I try not to look at any resemblance that he has to the man I love. I just focus on the red in his eyes and the red haze surrounding mine until all I see are sheets of crimson sparking across my vision, clouding everything. I hold my hand over his forehead and use the rest of my body to hold him down as he struggles beneath me. I don't stop seeing red. Even when I try to close my eyes, it bursts forth behind my eyelids. I faintly hear someone calling my name in the background but I don't stop. I take! I feel it coursing into my body like a drug, the evil that is in him. I keep taking!

The sound of footsteps approaching doesn't stop me. I don't stop until something is thrown at me and I'm flung to the ground, off Tony.

"Willow!" someone screams in my ear.

I realize that someone is on top of me. I struggle but I feel too weak and sick to give much of a fight.

"Stop, Willow. You have to stop," a man's voice says, holding me down.

I writhe beneath him. My whole body hurts; it feels like it's on fire. Inside I feel like slime is running through my veins. I cry out in pain. Right before I give myself up to the horrendous pain, a cooling sensation washes over me. Something is putting out the flames, like water on fire. I finally relax when the pain subsides, when the red fades from my vision. I open my eyes and find Alec hovering over me. His eyes full of concern and fear. The sound of other voices around us brings me back to reality.

Reality has its disadvantages. My stomach lurches when I realize what I just did. Tears burn my eyes and my breath is caught in my chest. My heart feels like a dagger has been slammed through it. "I killed him!" I say in utter horror. My eyes are wide with shock. I can't even blink. I'm paralyzed with fear. Fear for what I've done, what I will become.

Alec looks at me with such sadness that it breaks the remaining pieces of my soul in two. *I killed him. I killed Tony.* Tears fall as I lay there, motionless in shock by what I just did. The world fades as I let my sorrow drown me. I want to cease living. I can't take this. I can't...

I'm pulled into a sitting position between two people. They hold me between them. "It's going to be okay, Willow," Claire says as she strokes my hair. I stare off behind her, calling her bluff. It *will not* be okay.

I see Alec leaning over Tony. Several others surround him, trying to block my view. I hear someone say, "We have to get moving. They'll be coming after us soon!"

Alec turns and glares at the man that I vaguely recognize as one of Erik's men. Alec looks back down at Tony's lifeless body, which they have hidden from me. My mind tells me to breathe even though I don't want to. I want to stop breathing, just like Tony stopped breathing.

Claire continues to stroke my hair. Connor pats my shoulder, unsure of what to do. I don't close my eyes. I keep staring at Alec, hovering over Tony. His body is tense and I see his arms shaking. I wonder if he's shaking because of his anger towards me. For taking a life. For becoming a Reaper.

Then someone sits up beyond him. Alec starts trembling as he turns to look at me. He gives a shaky smile before he slumps to the side, leaving me a full view of Tony. My heart stops as I stare at him in disbelief. He's sitting up, his expression disoriented. When he looks at me, he comes to his senses. "Willow?" he whispers, in a state of confusion.

My hope turns to horror as I wonder if Tony's ghost has come back to haunt me. I barely notice the woman crouching over Alec, trying to heal him.

Tony is dead... Am I seeing ghosts now? Is this a new gift? What's wrong with Alec? Maybe I'm dead too.

Tony's eyes look different, they aren't red, but they aren't yellow either. He looks down at Alec and seems torn between making sure he's okay and coming to me.

"He's alive!" Claire exclaims in my ear. She shakes me.

Is he really alive? *How?* Claire and Connor both grab a hold under my arms and help me stand.

I walk shakily forward and Tony meets me in the middle. I look into his eyes. They are brown, flecked with bits of amber and a hint of green. I've never seen an eye color like this. *"I'm so sorry, Tony,"* I say to him in my head.

He doesn't look affected by my apology. I realize that he must not be able to hear me. I repeat it aloud. "I'm so sorry, Tony."

His face softens and he reaches out and pulls me

into him. "No, I'm the one that should be sorry, Willow. I tried..." He reaches a shaking hand to my head and pulls me tighter against him. "You saved me," he whispers.

"We have to go now!" Alec calls out.

We both turn to see that Alec's okay. He's back to normal. The sound of a helicopter's blades chopping through the night air approaches. I see the lights not far from where we are.

"They're coming," Tony says with surety.

We make sure everyone in our party is accounted for. Then we run. Alec leads the way. He takes us down several twists and turns of alleys. We have to stop and hide in the shadows of the buildings every few minutes to avoid the searchlights of the helicopters overhead. Tony keeps pace with the rest of the group but finds himself easily winded. I wonder what's wrong with him.

Eventually, we find ourselves out of the city area and in the middle of an open clearing. Up ahead, the familiar tree line of the forest greets us. I grab as many of the people as I can. Claire grabs a few, and the other people with us who have purple eyes grab the rest, turning our entire party invisible. We run through the clearing while the helicopters roar right past us, unable to see our group. I pray the whole time that no one in the helicopters has the gift Candy has. We can't risk having them see through our invisibility. We run, huddled together, for miles, until the sound of the helicopters are just a distant memory.

I shiver under the moonlight, noticing the weather has gotten even cooler. It's a weird feeling knowing this shouldn't be the case. Alec unzips his coat and drapes it over my shoulders. "Thanks," I whisper. He nods his head and moves up towards the front of our group.

Tony places his arm around me and squeezes. I tense up at his touch. He starts to loosen his grip, realizing that he's made me uncomfortable, so I quickly reach up, grab his hand, and lace it in mine. We both relax our posture. It's going to take a while to get used to the fact Tony's back to normal. He isn't going to turn all Zack zombie-monster on me again... Hopefully.

The walk back to Erik's camp is done mostly in silence. It takes us several hours in the dark to travel, but we eventually make it.

As soon as we set foot on the camp grounds, several of Erik's soldiers meet us and help us inside. Steaming hot chocolate is waiting in the mess hall, along with some dinner leftovers. I greedily take a cup and warm my hands. It has to be in the forties outside…far too cold for the thin jeans and t-shirt I'm wearing.

I'm thankful Alec lent me his jacket. I would have been an icicle before we got here had it not been for him. I eye him sitting at a table, talking with Marya. She looks relieved to see him. I begin to warm up, so I take the jacket off, walk over, and hand it to Alec. He gratefully accepts it and slips it back on.

"Thanks for keeping it warm," he playfully tells me.

I smile and try not to look at Marya and him awkwardly. "Thanks for aiding in the keep Willow warm project." That one gets a laugh out of Marya. I wave by to them and go in search of Tony.

I find Tony standing in a corner by himself. The others have given him a wide girth. I can feel the tension in the room and know it's partly due to his presence. I walk over to him, making sure to check his eyes before I wrap my hands around his middle. I hug him tightly, afraid to let him go. Afraid I'll lose him again.

"I'm not going anywhere," he tells me, kissing the top of my head.

Erik walks into the room and finds us. "Hey, Willow, can we speak for a minute in private?"

"Is that cool?" I ask Tony in my mind. He doesn't answer me. I look up at his eyes and he gives me that smile that says it's fine. I'm going to miss not being able to talk to him in our own private way. "I'll be right back," I say and squeeze Tony's middle before walking away.

Erik and I walk into his conference room. He closes the door and purses his lips. I can tell he's trying to figure out how to ask a question that's on his mind. He shifts his feet on the floor and hesitates. He opens his mouth, and then closes it a few times.

"Erik, whatever you have to say, just say it. I'm not going to get mad," I urge him.

He studies me for a moment and then says, "Okay..." He runs his hand through his dark hair. "I'm not comfortable having Tony here. I'm just being honest, Willow. I'm in charge of keeping a lot of people safe and I'm not sure if having him stay here is the best idea." He looks torn and relieved at the same time.

I was afraid he would feel this way. Erik is very protective of his people and he doesn't take strangers into his home easily. I think about my response for a minute before actually saying it. "I completely understand. Maybe it'll be a good idea to take Tony away for a few days to make sure all is well. Then, if he shows no signs of a relapse, we'll come back when we know all is safe."

He runs his hand under his chin in thought, and then nods his head. "Three days. If by the third day you haven't seen anything happen that would raise a red flag, you can bring him back here."

I nod. I think that's only fair and, honestly, it's a huge concession for Erik to make for me. "Can we at least stay here tonight?" I ask, even though I'm pretty sure of the answer.

Erik shakes his head.

He doesn't need to explain. I nod my head in silent understanding. I put my hand out to him and we shake on it. Erik opens the door for me and we walk back to the main room together.

I smile at Tony when I see him standing right where I left him. He greets me with open arms and I gladly accept them as they wrap around me. Looking up at him, I say, "We need to talk." A look of concern flashes across his features. "Don't worry, it's nothing bad," I assure him, although I guess it could be bad seeing as how we are going to go out on our own, while everyone else is out there hunting me down.

"Okay," Tony says. His tone shows me that he's still

worried. He looks at Erik, who doesn't look too happy to see him.

"Meet me in the hall?" I ask. "I need a quick second." He nods his head and exits the mess hall.

I grab Alec, Connor, and Claire really fast, and lead them out to the hall. Marya follows us out, probably because Alec naturally grabs her hand. I can't help but feel a little ping of annoyance. I guess I don't feel like she belongs in our little clique, but that seems mean, so I brush it off. I have to get used to her presence if they are going to be together.

We grab Tony along the way and I take them back to the room where Erik and I just were. We all take a seat at the small, circular table.

"Alright," I begin once the door's closed and I have everyone's attention. I notice Connor has taken his dinner plate in here with him and is nibbling on a chicken bone. I laugh inwardly and then get back to business. "I just spoke with Erik and he has some reasonable concerns he'd like me to address." Everyone waits expectantly so I continue. "I understand what Erik is saying. His main responsibility here is to keep everyone safe. He feels like that could be compromised if Tony were to stay here at the camp. And I have to agree with him to some extent." I glance over to Tony, who I can tell is battling between understanding and feeling hurt by my words. "Anyhow, we've hashed out a plan so we can get what we both want: he wants safety and I want Tony." My face heats up, realizing how that just sounded. I don't look at Tony when I continue, "The plan is this: Tony and I will go somewhere and stay there for three days. If Tony exhibits no signs or symptoms of being controlled by Zack, then we'll come back here."

I look up to see Tony's expression perk up. His emotions roll off him and I can't help but sense them. It's clear that he's excited, yet scared, about spending three days alone with me. He doesn't feel like Zack is going to take over again, but he can't help but feel like he isn't safe for me. Like a seesaw, the feelings switch back to excitement about having time with me alone. I try not to blush but fail miserably.

Alec intercedes, "I don't think that's such a good idea, Willow. I don't like the idea that you'll be with Tony alone. What if something happens and he returns to the way he was? If you're alone with him, you may not be able to defend yourself properly."

Marya crosses her arms defensively. I can tell she's slightly jealous at Alec's concern. This only makes me smile. I wipe it off my face quickly, to address Alec's fear.

Before I can speak, Claire chimes in. "I agree with Alec, Willow. He's right. I think it would be nice if we could all go somewhere together and just hang out for three days. God only knows I've needed a break and I'd love to spend time together like we used to. I miss having you all around."

"Yeah, vacation!" Connor adds, pointing his chicken bone at me.

My eyes perk up. That sounds really fun actually. Even if it's not just Tony and me, it will be Tony, me, and all of our closest friends. The friends I love will be with me... Oh, and Marya.

I nod my head to agree with Claire. "I like that idea." I turn to Tony. I'd been thinking that we could venture out and try to find Lee and our people. I'd love to see my father and Sabby to make sure they are alright. I'm sure Connor wants to see his family too. I know that's not the best move though. The last thing I need right now is to lead Zack and his army towards them. "Tony, do you think we'd be able to go to your old cabin by the lake for a few days? It's the only place I can think of that would be a good fit for our situation."

Tony begins to relax for the first time tonight. I believe in him, his friends believe in him, maybe now he believes in himself. He nods his head and with his cool demeanor says, "Yeah, I think we can arrange that."

All of us smile and agree to gather our things and meet back here in twenty minutes. Before we leave the room, I call to Alec, "Hey Alec, do you mind sticking around for a quick second. I need to talk to you alone."

Both Marya and Tony look a little uncomfortable, but they leave the room along with Connor and Claire.

Alec sits down next to me. "What's going on?" He looks at me with interested navy eyes.

I'm not sure where to start, but I know I need to tell Alec about his dad. "I saw your dad."

"Really?" he asks. His face is neither filled with excitement by the news or disappointment. It's something right in between the two emotions.

"Yes..." I look at him a bit uncomfortably and bite

my lip.

Alec leans in towards me. "I can tell you're nervous about saying something. What is it? Is he a Reaper?"

I shake my head sadly. "No, he's not a Reaper. He's connected with Zack. He helped him keep me hostage."

Alec's face contorts in anger. "Did he hurt you?" He puts his hand on mine.

I look down at our hands together. It doesn't feel romantic, it feels like a friend concerned over another friend's wellbeing. "He slapped me."

"What?" He slams his other fist down on the table.

I flinch. "He's not good, Alec." Tears come to my eyes as I think about how Blake treated me. I think about my own father and how I could never fathom him doing anything like Alec's father did. I know it will hurt for Alec to know this about his own flesh and blood, but he has to know.

Alec looks away from me for a moment, processing my words. I see his jaw clench. "I had a feeling he was in cahoots with Dr. Hastings..." He takes a deep breath and then turns to look at me. His eyes are filled with pain and betrayal. "I'm so sorry, Willow."

I put my hand on his this time and shake my head. "It's not your fault, Alec. You can't control your family. I just wanted you to know. I wouldn't feel right not telling you about it."

He nods his head sadly. "I'm glad you told me. If I see that old man, we are going to hash it out big time. I can't believe he hit you."

"Don't think about it, Alec. I'm safe now. I'm here. We don't need to worry about your father right now. Just know that if you see him, he's not to be trusted," I say.

"I know." Alec's shoulders are slumped. I pull him into a hug. His feelings are strong and I have a hard time filtering them out. It's one thing to be betrayed or disappointed by a person, but to have that person be your own father… it's something that cuts your heart, a deep bleeding gash type of cut. We hug each other as tight as we can, finding solace in our hold. When he pulls back, he sniffs and tries to blink away the moisture that's built in front of his eyes.

"We should go get ready," I tell him.

"Yes. Don't forget your coat." He tries but fails to find a smile.

"Definitely!" I stand up and allow him to lead me out of the room.

Tony stays with Erik, at Erik's request of course, while we go pack. It doesn't take long to get the few precious items I own. I pick up the flower ring Alec gave me so long ago. It has long since dried out, so the petals are very delicate. I put it back carefully in my journal and place it with the rest of the items in my backpack. Placing a hand in my back pocket, I feel my mother's letter tucked safely inside.

I run into Candy and Jake outside my room. "Hey, Willow," Candy says a little uncertainly.

"Hey, what's up?" I ask, even though I have an idea of what's up based solely on her emotions. I had asked

Claire to go and see if Candy wanted to come with us. I can tell that she's not ready for that yet.

"I hope you don't mind, but I can't go with you," she says. Then she raises an eyebrow. "I guess you already knew that, huh?"

I know how much she hates me using my gifts on her. Even if my eye color didn't give it away, Candy would always know what I'm doing. "Sorry..." I look down at my shoes and back up at her. "You are worried that Zack still has control of him, aren't you?"

She nods her head. "I still have a hard time processing how badly my brother treated me the last time. I don't ever want to see him or have any contact at all with him. He's just like my father."

"I understand. We are taking Tony away and we'll make sure that Zack has lost the ability to control him. I hope after that, you will be able to trust being around him again. I don't want that to hurt our friendship. Zack has already taken away too much from the two of us." I try not to let my emotions get even more heightened at the thought of how many people Candy's family has hurt.

Her eyes look sad as she nods her head. "I will. Please don't tell Tony though. I don't want him to feel bad. This has nothing to do with him."

"I won't say anything." I give her a hug. I'm glad that it's nowhere near as awkward as it used to be.

"Good luck, Willow," she says before she turns and links her hand with Jake's. He gives me a smile and a nod before they walk away. Jake's not a man of many words.

"Thanks," I call back at them.

I find Claire on my way to our assigned meeting spot and she links our arms. "This is going to be nice, three days of peace and quiet." She squeezes my arm and I can't help but feel a bit of excitement myself. Twenty minutes later, and not a second too soon, we're all assembled and ready to leave. Erik wishes us well as we set off towards the lake house.

The night is crisp and I'm thankful for the extra layers I bothered to put on. I look over at Marya as she shares a private joke with Alec. She giggles and hits his arm.

I feel a twinge of jealousy but it bypasses quickly as I slide my hand into Tony's. I can't help but notice how warm he is, even though outside it feels bitterly cold. We have to take several breaks to let Tony rest. I can tell everyone is getting tired, but Tony takes the cake. He tries to remain strong, but I can tell he doesn't act the way he used to...ever since I reaped all the powers from him. A twinge of guilt presses through me now that I realize the cause of the major change in Tony. I try to remind myself that I saved him and that was the cost of doing so. I didn't try to take all of his powers intentionally.

We arrive at the lake house right before dawn. The sky takes on pink and blue hues that reflect over the surface of the water. The mountains in the distance make for one of the most picturesque backgrounds. It's quite lovely. Tony goes around to a knot in one of the trees and emerges with a key. He unlocks the door and we all shuffle in.

We follow Tony into the living room and all but

collapse onto the furniture. Tony and I take the couch, Connor and Claire take the love seat, and Alec and Marya make a pallet on the floor. The second our eyes close, we're out.

NINE

I slowly inject the dark green liquid into Tony's vein.

My heart is accelerating at unnatural speeds, pounding in my ear, as I empty the entire syringe into his arm. I pray that this will work. There is too much at risk. Could he die because of this? I pick up the next needle. The thick, bright red liquid looks wrong. It's not normal, but I already know that its ingredients are more than they appear. Even still, I cringe as I bring it up to Tony's arm. "I love you," I tell him before I empty the contents into his bloodstream.

My eyes dart open and I stare up at the wooden rafters of Tony's log cabin, trying to regain composure. My heart is still beating hard in my chest.

Tony rustles a little next to me and opens his eyes. He looks around confused for a moment until his eyes land on media give him a warm smile and wrap my arms around him, letting him feel safe. This is the first time in a while that he's been able to wake up and not feel the threat of Zack looming over him.

"Morning," he says softly in a gruff voice.

"Morning." I nestle my head into the crook between his shoulder and neck. We lay like that for a while. His sent is intoxicating. As I breathe him in, I mentally try to will my heart to calm down. I'm starting to notice the differences between a vision and a dream. The visions have a slight haze around them. It is as if not everything around the story itself is permanent; it could be smudged out easily like an eraser would. But what did that mean? I hate to think of the ramifications to the contents of that red shot. I rub my eyes with a shaky hand. I decide not to tell Tony about it right away. Not until I know what it means.

I feel Tony shift beneath me and sit up. "How about we make a fire and get some grub going. I'm starving."

My eyes light up. I bite my lip. "Ramen?" I question, hoping that's what he has in mind.

He shakes his head playfully at me. "You're cracking me up, Willow. Yes, I'll get out some Ramen." I clap my hands almost a little too loudly, but I can't help it. The second he said we'd have Ramen, my salivary glands went into overdrive.

Tony and I quietly put on our shoes and slip out the front door. He brings his ax with him so he can chop some wood. I help him gather the weathered logs next to the house while he chops them down to size. I can tell he tires out quickly. The way he swings the ax now looks like it takes much more effort than before. I think about stepping in and taking over, but knowing Tony would never want to hand in his man card, I think better of it. Before long, we both have handfuls of wood to carry back to the lake house.

Tony carries about half of what I carry and I can tell by his grumbling that it makes him more than peeved.

135

I try to ignore his comments that aren't aimed at me, but at himself. More and more, I start stacking on the guilt though. I know that he'd have no problem doing these seemingly simple tasks if it weren't for me. We stack the wood on the front porch and take a few pieces in with us to start the fire.

When we get back inside, everyone is starting to wake up. Connor looks like his back hurts from sleeping so awkwardly, while Claire has her head in the crook of his shoulder. She's still fast asleep. He shakes her shoulder and she wakes with a start. I laugh to myself, thinking that Connor would be a pretty comfortable pillow.

I place the logs in the fire and Tony sets to light them with a piece of paper and flint stone. I find it fascinating to watch him make the fire start.

Once the flames are in full swing, we warm our hands over the fire and the others move closer to join us. Marya takes a seat next to me, still wrapped in one of Tony's quilts. Alec places his hands on either side of her to help warm her up. *How nice of him...*

I stand up and volunteer to go to the well and fetch water. Tony stands as well, not wanting me to be alone. I give him a half smile. It's sweet, really.

I hold his hand, placing the bucket in my other. The birds chirp overhead and then fall silent. A cold wind blows past us, making me shiver. "Smells like snow," Tony says simply.

"Snow?" I question. After getting myself psyched up about Project ELE and the whole, 'warming the earth to unlivable temperatures', it makes no sense at all. It's hard to wrap my mind around it.

Tony stops me by tugging gently on my arm. I turn to face him. The wind blows my hair and a few strands stick to my frozen face. Tony reaches up and carefully tucks it behind my ears. His fingers graze my cheek. "You're so beautiful," he says simply. My gaze drops as my shy side sets in. Any time someone is that frank with me, it throws me for a loop. He doesn't let my gaze wander long before his index finger brings my chin back up to face him. "In my wildest dreams I never thought that I would be able to be near you again without the fear of hurting you. "The pain he felt is apparent in his brown eyes. I open my mouth, but he holds his hand up to stop me from speaking. "I need to say this first. I'm so sorry, Willow. I thought that being attacked by my parents, and then seeing them killed, would be the worst thing I'd ever be forced to go through. This...this was excruciating." His eyes water ever so slightly. "There were times that I blacked out the episodes where Zack controlled me. I was grateful for the times I blacked out. But...the times that killed me," he pounds his chest with his fist, "were when I was aware of Zack controlling me. I saw you through his eyes. I tried to fight but no matter how hard I tried to fight him, he won. I thought about taking my life..."

"No, Tony!" My eyes are pooled with tears now.

He holds his hand up again, asking me to let him finish. The emotion on his face is more than I can bear, but I let him continue. "I thought about it but I couldn't live with myself if I took the easy way out. I knew Zack would just find another person to do his bidding. I promised myself that I would fight every day if I had to, in order to come back to you eventually." He grabs my hand in his. "Will you ever be able to forgive me for what I did to you?"

I wipe my eyes with my fingertips and smile gingerly at him. "I can't." A crushed look overcomes his features. I shake my head quickly. "No wait, that's not what I mean! I meant that I don't need to forgive you, Tony. It wasn't *you* that hurt me. I never once thought it was you or blamed you for what happened. I knew it was that monster controlling you. There's no reason to accept your apology because you've done nothing wrong. You were a victim." He opens his mouth but I pull a Tony and raise my hand to stop him. "I need to say this first." I give him a half grin and I watch him relax a small bit when I start talking again. "I never thought for a second I would lose you forever. Sometimes it seemed that all hope was lost, but I never let it slip permanently from my grasp. I love you, Tony. I always will, no matter what. I am so thankful that somehow you came back to me…even if it meant I had to reap the one thing you probably loved most about yourself. "The last part comes out in almost a whisper as I admit to something I've tried to suppress ever since I reaped his powers. The guilt tries to consume all of me and I try to hold on to the fact that had I not done that, he may have been gone from me forever. *But what if I didn't stop there? What if I killed him?* Those are the questions that haunt me.

Tony shakes his head defiantly. "If you think that

losing my powers was worse than not being able to have you, then you have it all wrong. Willow, I would have done anything to get back to you. Cut off my limbs, take away my sight, let me hear no longer...that would have been a better existence than losing you."

My heart wants to scream at this man before media can't be worth all of that...*can I?* I'm just a single person in this huge world. A little fish in a big pond. How could I mean that much to him? Or to anyone for that matter? I drop the bucket at my feet and wrap my arms around Tony, making sure not to squeeze too tight. I close the distance and let my lips meld to his. Tony wastes no time returning my declaration of love.

"I love you," I say between our kisses.

He places his hand on the back of my head and forces me closer. We kiss deeper than ever before and my stomach dances in rhythm. Cool flakes of snow dance off my cheeks. Just being with Tony makes me feel so warm inside that I swear I can hear the flakes sizzle when they touch my skin. We break apart at the same time, opening our eyes.

We both look up at the sky and are met with falling snow, the first I've seen in a long time. I stick my tongue out and let the snowflakes fall in my mouth. The cool sensation makes me think of ice cream.

I look back at Tony, who's apparently been watching me this whole time with a funny smile. "Beautiful," he mutters, kissing me lightly on the lips. I return his kiss with one of my own.

"We better go get the water before someone comes looking for us," Tony says jokingly. I pick up the pail and grab Tony's hand; together we draw water from the well.

When we open the front door, swirls of snow drift in with us. We hurry in and I place the heavy bucket of water on the floor, while Tony closes the door. We both b-line it for the fire, rubbing our hands over the warmth.

"How far did you have to go?" Alec asks.

I bite my lip, trying not to let him see my smile. "You know...it's a little ways," I say, hoping he takes my vague answer and doesn't question me further. I don't dare look his way though, because I know he'll see right through my façade.

Claire gives me the look. You know, the one where she knows what's going on, even if no one else does.

I try to hide my smile but fail miserably.

"Let's get some grub," Tony says, changing the subject. I should have known he'd have my back.

No one bats their eyes at the mention of food. Connor and Alec help Tony prepare the food 'for the girls' as they said. I find it humorous to see the guys in the kitchen while the girls are parked in the living room by the fire. The only thing I'm not so sure about is sitting shoulder to shoulder with Marya. *Oh, how this girl gets to me.* If she starts asking for relationship advice though...I'm outta here.

Claire opens up the curtains so we can watch the falling snow. It's falling heavier than it was before and the world is already beginning to be covered in a blanket of white. We are all mesmerized by it. With the virus spreading so rapidly, it was always suggested that we stay indoors when the temperatures dropped. They said that the cold could lower your immune system. In times like that, a vulnerable immune system was the kiss of death. Now that I doubt I will have to worry about the virus again, I wonder if we could go out and play in the snow like I always wanted to do as a kid.

"So," Marya says, breaking the silence and my chain of thoughts. "This is a nice cabin."

We all look around awkwardly at the furnishings and nod our heads. *Who am I kidding?* This friendship with Marya will never work. I sigh, prompting Claire to ask what's wrong. "OH, nothing," I say. But she knows; she's my best friend after all.

Marya sits next to me and fidgets with her hands. We fall into another awkward silence.

I gaze back out at the forest that has become a winter wonderland. Large snowflakes float down through the trees. It seems so peaceful. How can anything go wrong when there is such beauty outside? "I wonder if we can make one of those men made of snow later, if this weather lasts," I say.

"I think you mean a snowman," Marya corrects me.

Did she seriously just do that? I do my best to keep from turning and glaring at her.

Before long, the guys come over to where we're sitting. They distribute bowls of yummy goodness.

My stomach jumps, knowing what it's about to

receive. "Mmmm, Ramen," I say savoring the smell.

"Raman has a lot of MSG. I try not to make a habit of eating it," Marya says.

Oh good grief, just eat it. It's free! By the time I'm done with my second bowl, I feel bad asking for a third. *Only if there are leftovers*, I tell myself.

Well, turns out there were no leftovers…after Marya sucked down her fourth bowl.

Tony sees my annoyance and takes my hand, pulling me to my feet. "How about we get settled?" he asks. I try not to smile but fail miserably. I nod my head.

He takes me upstairs to his old room and we put our packs down on the floor. Tony falls back onto his old bed, "Ahh, home sweet home."

I can't help but smile. He looks so carefree and… cute. He pats the bed next to him. I gladly oblige and cuddle up beside him. Tony plays with my hair as I lay my head on his chest, feeling his heart beating beneath me. My hand runs along his abs trying to figure out if he has a six-pack or twelve-pack.

A quiet voice breaks though my thoughts and I still myself, trying to hear it. "Do you hear that?" I ask Tony. It's almost like I've picked up some kind of radio wave.

He lifts his head from the bed and raises his eyebrow at me. "Hear what?"

I guess that answers my question. I sit up on the bed and focus on hearing the noise again, but I come up short. "That was weird. It was like I was picking up a radio signal or something. I could hear some man talking, but it was muffled, like it was far away. That was bizarre. Now it's gone."

"Hmm, yeah that is strange." He pulls my arm so that I will have to lie back down.

I settle my head on his chest again and listen to the pounding of his heart. I lift my head up and grin at him. "You do know that I'm not sleeping in here tonight, right?"

He laughs. "I wouldn't ask you to do anything so dishonorable."

"Mmhmm." I see the mischief in his eyes that tells me he wouldn't send me downstairs either. We've fallen asleep beside each other before, but to be alone in a room all night would be pushing the limits.

He holds his hands up. "Seriously."

I stop giving him my fake stern look. "I know you aren't like that, Tony." I push him gently on the shoulder.

He tickles me playfully and I let out a squeak. "So, are you ready to go make those men made out of snow?"

"Ah! You were listening!" I catch his hands before he can tickle me again.

"I couldn't help it. You looked so captivated." He smiles.

"Did your parents let you play out in it when you were younger?" I ask him.

A mix of emotions crosses his face. "Yes, my parents occasionally let me go out in it. I would only get twenty minutes or so, but it was enough for me to enjoy myself."

Anxious to change the subject so he doesn't have to dig up the past, I say, "So, are you ready? I think I'm going to make a woman made of snow. Or a snow angel!" My eyes light up with excitement.

"You are super cute when you get all worked up, you know?" He sits up and puts on the shoes that he'd kicked off his feet before lying down.

"Yes, I know that," I joke. I grab his arm and we hustle down the stairs. The living room is empty. I look out the window and find that everyone else has already beaten us to the punch.

We put our jackets on, Tony lets me borrow an old one of his moms that's waterproof, and we head outside. The cold air makes my cheeks burn, but in a good way. We walk down the few steps to meet up with everyone who's already having a blast.

Claire laughs when Alec pummels Connor in the face with a snowball. Connor squints his eyes at him. "Hey, the face is off limits!" he says, circling his face dramatically with his index finger. He tries to throw a snowball back at Alec but his aim is horrible and it glides past him and hits a tree.

"You throw like a girl!" Alec jokes with Connor.

"Don't talk to my boyfriend like that!" Claire says in more of a joking tone than a serious one. She goes to Connor's side and pats his shoulder. "Did he hurt your feelings, babe?" she asks in a pouty, over-dramatic voice.

Connor hangs his head in mock shame. Then he grabs Claire and together they go falling backwards on the snow, giggling. After a little wrestling, they start making snow angels.

Alec goes over to help Marya make her 'snow-man'. There is a good amount of snow on the ground, but not enough to make a full-sized man. Instead, they make a miniature snow family.

I try not to roll my eyes. I don't know why she is bothering me. I need to find a way to get over myself. I know she's not a bad girl.

"You can hit her," I hear someone say, not just anyone, Zack.

I whirl around. My hearts starts accelerating as I look around for my arch nemesis.

"Willow, what's wrong?" Tony grabs ahold of my shoulders. I keep darting my head this way and that, trying to find out where he's hiding.

"He's here," I tell him.

Tony's eyes widen. "Zack?"

I nod my head.

"Ah, I wondered how you pulled it off. You little reaper, you!" Zack says again.

I move out of Tony's grip and run towards the lake. "Where are you, Zack? Show yourself!"

He laughs menacingly and it echoes inside my head. "I'm here."

"Where?!" I yell.

"By that canoe," he says.

I run over to the canoe that's upside down on the grass. Where Tony must have left it before he came after me. There's nothing there. "Don't play games with me, you little bastard!"

"I'm not exactly little, or a bastard. My dad was very much in my life, unfortunately. Maybe I'm in the water? You should swim in and try to find me," he says.

I realize that something, other than his stupid idea, is off. He sounds way too clear. If he's hiding out here and calling to me, then I wouldn't hear him this easily.

Tony runs up to me. "Willow! Is he really here?" He turns me in his arms so I have to look at him.

I try to look around him to find where that sneaky monster is hiding.

Tony's eyes widen and he grabs my chin and forces me to look at him. "Your eyes are red! You need to calm down now!" he orders me.

I shake my head. My eyes are red? Usually the red blurs my vision, but I don't see it. Then it clicks. "I can hear him because he's in my head!" I take a deep breath. Tony looks confused. "Could you hear him talk to you in your head?"

"What do you mean?" he asks, still not following my thought process.

"Did you hear him when he tried to control you?" I point to my head.

His eyes widen with realization. "You took it from me. You took whatever sick power, or weakness, whatever he gave me that made me susceptible to his control." Fear washes over him. "No, no, no! He's going to be able to control you now. Now he can make you go right to him."

"Never!" I say.

"Hey, that's a great idea. Why don't you come to me

right now, Willow," Zack says inside my head.

I feel a strange pull. "And where exactly are you?" I ask him in my head. Tony gives me a strange look but I hold up my hand to keep him from asking.

"Ha! Good try, Sugar. Why don't you just start heading North? Leave your friends there if you want to keep them safe," Zack says cockily.

That strange pull tries to make me move my feet. I resist it. "No," I tell him. Then I focus on blocking him out. I can feel a wall slowly being pulled down between our connection, until, finally, I can't sense Zack any longer.

Tony looks at my eyes. "Silver?" he asks. "What does that do?" He was there when we met Jennifer, but at the time, we didn't know the extent of what she was able to do.

"I can block people's powers," I say. I can't help but feel utterly creeped out still. Zack has a way of leaving a slimy impression on me; making me feel like I need a shower. "We should go back," I tell him. A sick feeling is churning in my stomach.

He nods his head and we jog back to the cabin. I don't see my friends anywhere. "Alec?" I call out. "Clarie, Connor?" Nobody answers. "Marya?" I ask. Nobody answers me. My heart starts pounding in my chest like a drum.

"They're probably inside," Tony says, trying to calm me down.

I have a really bad feeling about this. We run up to the door. Nobody is on the first floor. Tony runs upstairs.

"Nobody up there," Tony says as he comes back down. "Maybe they're hiding?"

"I don't know, Tony. I have a bad feeling about this." I try to open up my mind. Maybe I can sense their emotions. I feel a small taste of fear but then it stops short. It's completely gone and I can't feel anything else except for Tony's concern for me. "Something happened!" I tell him.

Tony runs to grab his bag. He pulls out a pistol and checks that it's loaded. Then he nods silently and we both run back outside. I try calling for them again and again but I don't get any responses. It's like they vanished. We comb the area around the cabin and we both spot the footprints at the same time. There are several of sets of them leading towards the front of the house from the woods and back into the woods again. There were footprints all over the front area of the cabin because everyone was playing in the snow. These footprints are different though. They look like military boots and several sets of them by the looks of it.

My stomach drops as I see a few smaller shoe prints heading into the woods. "Claire," I whisper, knowing that's the only person these footprints could belong to.

Tony raises his gun as we follow the prints into the forest. I see an area where it looks like there was a scuffle. Then it looks like someone was dragged through the snow. We follow the trail for several yards until we arrive at a paved roadway covered in snow. The footprints stop where the tire tracks begin.

My breathing quickens, as does my panic. I look all around me and listen intently. I have to find them…I just have to. I let the shield down in my head and then say, "Zack, if you had anything to do with this, I *will* kill you." I slap the shield back up without waiting for an answer. "We've got to go. We have to find Erik and get his reinforcements to help before it's too late."

Tony agrees and, without a word, we run back to the house to get our stuff. As soon as we get there, I shoot up the stairs only to turn back and see Tony at the bottom, catching his breath. "Tony, we have to hurry," I say desperately.

His face is masked with pure frustration when he looks at me. "I'm sorry; I'm just not as fast as you are anymore.

My face falls. I just made him feel like crap for the one thing *I* took from him. "It's okay. I'll hold your hand and give you some of my ability when we run back or give you a piggyback ride if I have to. We just need to move quickly." He nods his head but I can feel a huge lump of broken pride rolling off him. The pain is evident in his face. He feels helpless and afraid; afraid mostly that he'll lose me because of his weakness. It angers me to no end to know that's how he feels. I never stopped loving him when he was a Reaper…why would I stop now?!?

Just as quickly as we entered, we leave again with our bags in tow. I take Tony's hand in mine. If I can transfer my invisibility to people or help someone walk through a wall just by touching them, I have to be able to help him run faster. I focus my power as we start out at a fast-paced jog, towards the camp. We increase our speed slowly and before I know it, we are darting through the forest.

I look over at Tony. "It worked," I say as we run through the snow-covered trees. Hoping this helps him feel less powerless.

He gives me a slight smile and then focuses on the path ahead of us. I need to figure out how to get Tony his gift back sooner, rather than later. It takes us a little over an hour to reach Camp Cheley.

We walk through the gate and unlike the many times that the camp appeared deserted, today it's the opposite. Throngs of people are gathered in front of the doors to the Commons. We waste no time and run up to see what's going on. I can feel the heightened emotions of everyone around us, weighing me down like an anvil. Fear, nervousness, frustration, and more seep out of the people and come rolling off towards me.

I turn that gift off so I can better focus on the situation at hand. That's when I realize that the majority of the people outside have yellow eyes, except for Candy. I find her in the crowd, sticking out like a sore thumb. She looks lost and utterly panicked.

I look around the group of recognizable faces. "Lee!" I call out from behind the crowd. Everyone's eyes turn towards Tony and me. The crowd parts and I can see Erik and Lee talking to each other quietly in the front of the group. Tony tries to move in front of me, but I squeeze his hand, hinting to him to stay still, that I'm alright.

I cringe when Erik looks at us, knowing that we are breaking our deal. I brought Tony back before the three days was up. He doesn't look mad though. No, his eyes are filled with…sympathy. I look from him to Lee and notice they both share the same sad expression. *Something is wrong; something is really wrong.*

"No," I whisper as I walk towards them. My whole body is shaking and Tony instinctively wraps a protective arm around me. *No... My dad, Sabby.* Something is wrong, I feel it, I know it. Why else would they be looking at me that way?

"Willow," Lee says to me in a sad voice.

"What happened?" I ask, not dancing around the bush. I try to stand up taller. If I can fake that I'm strong enough to hear what he has to tell me, then maybe I won't crumble. Maybe I'll survive this just like every other time I've received awful, life-changing news.

"They've been taken," Lee tells me. I've never seen him so broken and hurt. It makes me weak in my knees.

My shakes turn into all out trembling. I thought they were safe with Lee. I shouldn't have left them. It's my fault; I should have protected my family. My brain runs a million miles a minute. A red haze starts overtaking my vision as I think about the unfairness of this horror show that has become my life. Will I always be destined to lose the ones I care about, to have my heart broken into a thousand pieces? When will this vicious cycle end? Just when I pick up a few pieces off the ground, they are blown to smithereens again! I close my eyes so they don't see them turning red.

I hear Tony telling them about Alec, Marya,

Connor, and Claire being taken. I lose myself and can't hear him talking anymore.

"It's not working," Erik says from far, far away. I feel him grab my hand in his.

A gentle wave of calm rolls over me. The red disappears from behind my eyelids. I breathe in and open my eyes. "Thank you," I tell him. If I have any hope of helping them, I have to remain calm and levelheaded. I turn to Lee with the newfound calmness that Erik has lent me. "Did you see who took them? Where they went?"

He shakes his head. "We don't know where they went, but we do know how they were taken. There were witnesses who saw it." His face still looks sad. "Well, actually, in a way they helped the kidnappers."

My hands are still trembling so I clasp them together, impatient to hear the story so I can get on with saving my family. "Somebody helped them take my dad and brother? Who?"

"Well, one of them was the boy you saved, John," Lee says.

My mind starts processing through everyone I've met recently. "A thirteen-year-old boy aided the kidnapping?" I ask in complete shock. I remember his gold eyes and all of the cuts he had from falling into the thorn bushes.

He nods his head. "Yes, but he was being controlled by Zack. When he came to, he told us everything he knew," Lee says.

"And the other person?" Tony asks for me.

"Peter," Lee says.

"I don't remember anyone named Peter," I say. The frustration is starting to triumph again within me.

"That's because you haven't met him yet." He catches my glare so he continues. "We found him recently, when we went back to the prison to try to find a way to communicate with the other shelters. We didn't see him come up on us until after we had the radio working and we finally made contact with the D.O.D. While invisible, he snuck in right in front of us and cut the lines. When our guys finally realized what happened, they grabbed him. After Peter became visible again, we saw his eyes change from red to purple."

"And what? You brought him home to live with you?" I ask, trying to keep my anger at bay.

"It's not like that, Willow. We couldn't leave him outside, just like we couldn't leave John alone. They are both good people. You know just as well as me that they had no choice in doing what Zack made them do." He turns to Tony and says, "Right?"

"Leave Tony out of this!" I yell. My face is on fire, despite the icy air that stings my cheeks.

Lee does a good job of masking the hurt expression on his face. "Look, I know you're upset, but we did what we thought was right. We controlled them as best as we could, and basically kept them locked up the entire time. We did everything we could."

"You didn't do enough!" I yell. Tony puts his hand on my shoulder, trying to calm me down, but I brush it

153

off. I don't want to be coddled right now. I want my family and friends.

"Look, we aren't getting anywhere arguing. You need to know that all that John and Peter did was find a way to get Zack's men inside our safe house undetected. Even if they weren't there, Zack would have found a way to get to them anyway," Lee tells me, trying to keep his cool.

He has a point. Zack found a way to take my friends right out from under my nose. I can't blame John or this Peter guy for that. I clench my fists. Out of the corner of my eye, I can see Erik moving in closer to me. My anger begins subsiding. "Okay, so did John and Peter tell you where they took my family?"

"No, they don't know where Zack was taking them." He pulls something out of his pocket. An envelope. "We came to look for you as soon as we could. They left this envelope with John." He hands it to me.

My heart is sinking as I reach for it. I half expect it to bite me or burn my fingers, but it doesn't. It's a simple white envelope. My name is scrawled across it in dark letters. Beneath it a cautionary note states: If you want them back safe, then this is for Willow's eyes only.

I look up at Tony, who looks like he wants to punch something. I can feel that his anger isn't from my brush off. It's all directed at Zack.

"Let's go inside," Erik says to us. He leads Tony and me inside. Lee follows us, but everyone else remains outside in the cold.

Erik lets me go into the small conference room.

"We'll give you a minute," he says.

Tony doesn't part from my side as I enter the room. "Do you want me to leave?" he asks me hesitantly.

I gently shake my head. "No, you can stay." We both take a seat at the table. Erik gives us some privacy and leaves the room.

Tony pulls a knife out of his back pocket. He hands it to me, but my hands are shaking too badly.

Making sure the wall in my mind is still up so Zack can't see me, I hand the envelope to Tony. "You open it, please," I say, disregarding the cautionary note on the front. I watch him insert the blade between the folded tab. He slices it quickly and puts his blade away. Pulling out a letter out from within the envelope, he hands it to me.

I slowly unfold it. This feather-light paper feels like a million pounds in my hands. The note is short and written in bolded ink.

Dear Willow,

My, my, you really are quite a handful, sugar. I should have known better than to think I could contain such a powerful creature. Thank goodness, you still have a weakness, my dear...

I hold some mighty powerful cards in my hand. Your family and friends are safe with me for now... As you know, the stakes are much higher in this game. I tire of our usual round of hide and seek. This time you will come to me. In addition, you WILL tell me how you came upon your powers. I'm sorry, did I say tell? I meant that you will show me how you came upon your powers.

Don't get any clever ideas about lying to me either, darling. I've heard through the grapevine that you wiped your boy toy's slate clean. Bring him with you and we will test out our little experiment on him first.

Tick, Tock. Time is of the essence since we still need the light of day to test our experiment. Meet me in my father's old lab before 2 p.m.

Oh, and if you don't want your loved ones to become a Reaper snack, then I suggest you and Tony come alone. My men will be keeping a close eye on the area. If they see anything fishy, your little brother will be the first to go.

PS: Sabby has your same curls.
Love Always,
Zack
XXXXX

My stomach is twisted in sick knots. I hold the paper out to Tony without looking at him. He takes it and reads it quickly, then he crumples it in his hand and slams his fist on the table. "Bastard!" he yells. I may have taken the power out of Tony but his willpower is still intact.

"You don't have to come." This isn't his family or his friends really. He has no reason to risk his life for them. "You shouldn't come," I clarify before I look up at him. I could never ask something like that out of anyone, not even Tony.

His eyes are on fire. "That's crap and you know it! Do you really think that I'd leave you at a time like this? That I'd just let Zack hurt the people you care about?"

"No, I know that you wouldn't, Tony. You've been through enough for me already. You aren't becoming the next lab rat," I say boldly, even if I feel less than strong right now.

"Willow, you are a part of me now. How long will it take you to understand this? I will go to the ends of the world for you and if that includes turning into a science experiment, then that's a price I'm willing to pay. I *am* going with you. I *will* kill Zack and we *will* get your family back." There is rage in his tone as he insinuates the verbs. I know it's not directed at me but I can feel the strength of it circling through the room. Like smoke before it erupts into fire.

There's a knock on the door and before I can say anything, it opens. Morgan and Audrey walk into the room, holding hands. Both of them look beyond tired. They take a seat across from Tony and me.

Audrey looks at me with sadness in her copper eyes. She grabs a thin, black box out from her jacket pocket and slides it across the table to me. "It was my sister's. She didn't survive long enough to use it."

Both Tony and I recognize what it is immediately. Tony grabs ahold of the box first and flips it open. Inside are two needles. One contains a neon-yellow liquid and the other, a bright red liquid.

Tony grabs for the yellow shot and I immediately grab his hand to stop him. "No."

Tony looks at me. "If we are going in there, I'm going to need my strength back," he says fiercely.

"She's right," Audrey says. We both look up at her as she continues. "You need to remain a clean slate. You can work with this if you do it right. The only needle you need to take with you is the red one." She reaches for the box and Tony lets her take it. "I didn't see far enough along to know if it will work or not, but it's your only hope right now," she says as she pulls the red shot out of the box and hands it to Morgan.

"You will have to find a way to switch it out with the one Zack will have. In Audrey's vision, the only person with the opportunity to switch it will be Tony. Willow, you will have to distract Zack." He flicks the liquid vial with his finger. I notice that no bubbles float to the top like usual. It looks different than what I'd seen before, yet, familiar.

"I had a vision about this," I say, remembering the moment that I noticed the liquid was different before I injected it into Tony.

Morgan nods his head and pushes his shades up further on his nose before continuing. "This is only a fraction of the immunization. The remainder is corn syrup and red food coloring. I saw your memories about how you suspect this is the way you got your gifts. I guess we will find out soon enough."

I scrunch my eyebrows. "I don't understand the corn syrup though. Why wouldn't I just inject Tony with a small amount?" My eyes widen as it dawns on media know Zack is going to want to use a syringe identical to Tony's to make sure I'm not trying to trick him. Having the corn syrup guarantees it will look as if his shot contains the full amount of red serum. Which means, when Zack gets his dose... "We are going to kill Zack," I say my conclusion aloud. The thought makes me ill, to the point of wanting to vomit. But why? I hate Zack; I can say that with absolute certainty. But kill him? I'm not so sure.

Morgan nods his head. "This may be your only chance and he has to be stopped."

Tony grabs my hand as I nod solemnly. I don't like the idea of taking another life but he is threatening my family. Any monster who would throw a four-year-old out to a den of Reapers, doesn't deserve to continue on this earth. But is it my place to take his life?

I hadn't realized that Erik and Lee walked in until Erik answers for me. "It *is* necessary," he tells me after having sensed my torn emotions.

I ask in desperation, "Are we sure that the entire

shot will kill him? What if he becomes a Reaper?"

"Then I'll take him out myself," Tony tells me. Then he looks at Audrey and Morgan. "I don't understand though, why we would need to go through such an elaborate scheme to get rid of Hastings? Why can't I just shoot him?"

Audrey answers. "He is controlling many people."

"Like he controlled me?" Tony asks.

Audrey shakes her head. "No, he used his compulsion to brainwash them. If you kill him, he has instructed his puppets to kill everyone and then to take their own lives in return. The connection will be severed the instant he is dead but his final instruction will not disappear as easily. He instructed his people to do this only if you kill him. He didn't say anything to them about what to do if he dies of his own accord. You stand a better chance of surviving this way and also to save the lives of the innocent people he's taken," she says. Morgan places the red needle in the case and pushes it back across the table.

"We should leave now," Tony says as he grabs the box.

I nod my head and stand. "Lee..." I know he's going to want to be our backup. He doesn't have to say anything for me to see it.

He holds his hands out. "They already told me. I don't have to like it, but I know that you have to do this alone. We'll wait here. But if you aren't back before nightfall, we're coming after you."

"Thank you," I tell him. I look over at Erik, Morgan, and Audrey. "Thank you all again. I hope this will work."

"We do too," Morgan says honestly. "Oh and Willow?"

I look at him. "Your secret is safe with us." He reaches out and takes my hand, giving it a squeeze of reassurance.

I know he means my secret, as to how I got my powers, is safe. I believe him. With our goodbye's said, Tony and I leave the camp with only a pistol each and a needle filled mostly with red corn syrup in our possession.

TEN

The sun is at its highest point in the sky, which tells me that it's either noon or somewhere shortly after.

I hold Tony's hand as we run towards the mountain. There's no time to dilly-dally. My family, friends, and everyone I intimately care about are being held hostage in that mountain. Thoughts of Sabby crying for me cause knots to form in my stomach. I bend forward slightly as we run, to make them go away. If I have any chance of doing this and doing this right, I can't be thinking of my little brother.

"There are going to be a lot of Reapers inside," I tell him. A chill runs up my spine as I think about the sick, twisted, vision I had not too long ago, about them making their home in the charred remains of our old shelter.

"How do you think Zack got inside with everyone?" he asks.

"I don't know. When we get to the tree line I plan on making us invisible, but we have to be ready for the attack," I tell him.

He nods his head. He's breathing heavily, but he's still keeping up with me. I can't use my full strength to propel us as fast as we could go. I need to save it for when we get there. I notice the trees thinning out. The snow has begun falling again, blurring our vision up ahead. I squeeze his hand and we stop before making it to the clearing.

He places his hand on my cheek. "No matter what happens, I want you to know that I love you." Snowflakes coat his hair.

"I love you too," I whisper. *So badly it hurts.*

He pulls me into his arms and kisses me passionately. I lean into him and let this horrible world fade away for a second. I need this moment to get me through what's coming next.

He's stronger than he knows, I think to myself as I open my eyes. He curls a strand of my hair around his finger before kissing me again, softer this time. I can't let anything bad happen to him; he means too much to me.

The pressure is on as we turn towards the mountain. I grab his hand again and turn us invisible. We jog at Tony's pace towards the shelter, which feels like a snail's pace compared to earlier.

Every nerve ending in my body is on heightened alert as we approach the shelter's doors. I anticipate seeing a thousand red eyes staring at us, but I see nothing. The stench of charred remains hits both of us as we reach the entrance. Tony nearly gags. I, having experienced it before in a vision, knew what to expect. I rub his back with my free hand. He rights himself quickly, trying desperately to hold onto his strong-persona image. His strength may be gone but he's still one of the brightest crayons in the box.

We take a moment to listen before we enter. I can hear some type of strange noise in the distance, but I'm not sure what it is. A high-pitch beeping accompanies the noises. It hurts my head at first, but then after a few seconds the pain disappears.

Before we walk in, Tony looks at me strangely. "Your eyes are silver and purple," he whispers.

I raise an eyebrow at him but respond since I don't know exactly what to say. I focus on keeping us invisible as we walk into the darkened hallway. The strange noises increase the further we walk, but the beeping sound never returns.

Nausea rolls around in my stomach and I wonder if Tony is as nervous as I am. In this moment, I'm not sure if I'm more scared of the Reapers or Zack. I would probably have to go with the Reapers due to their sheer numbers.

Only a few steps from the common area, the noise grows loud enough for me to recognize it. The sound of wailing cries echo out from the cavernous room. My heart sinks. I'm too late! Is it already past two? "He's hurting them!" I cry out and start running towards the opening to the room.

Tony grabs my hand and pulls me back. "No! It could be a trick," he says. "There are too many voices for this to be your friends and family. Plus, he said to meet him in his father's lab. Is the lab close by?"

I shake my head, hoping he's right. He pulls his pistol out of his back pocket. I pull mine out too. We remain invisible as we quietly approach the common area.

164

"What the?" Tony says as we walk into the room.

My breath whooshes out of me as I take in the sight. Reapers are lying everywhere, covering the floor. Some are curled into the fetal position and some are hunched over on top of the charred remains of the tables. Others are lying flat on their faces. The howling and moans are almost too much to endure. They writhe about in horrible pain... deep, unadulterated, excruciating pain.

I have to drop my invisibility and focus everything within me to block out their feelings. The air of emotions in this room is so thick that it attempts to suffocate me.

"He must have his father's device," Tony says.

I can't open my mouth or speak; I'm focusing too hard to keep them out. Tony senses my struggle and grabs my elbow, pulling me through the room. We have to step over the Reapers, who try, but fail miserably, at grabbing ahold of our feet. They are too weak to grasp anything within their hands. I nearly trip over a man who is crying so loudly that it reverberates in my ears. Tony steadies me and keeps moving me forward.

We reach the hallway with the bank of elevators. The metal doors are black from fire. Continuing down the hallway, we have to walk over a few more Reapers. Thankfully, we run into less and less as we walk. I start being able to regain my bearings again. "Do you know where you're going?" I ask him when I finally find my voice.

He stops and looks at me. "No. I just knew I had to get you away from there. Your eyes were swirling with silver and black. I knew that whatever was happening to you was pretty bad."

"It was hard to block out all of their emotions. There were simply just too many of them," I tell him even though he is quite aware of their numbers. There had to be over a hundred of them in that room alone.

"Do you know how to get to the lab?" he asks me.

I nod my head. "Yes." I grab his hand and we melt through the floor slowly. Tony looks at me with wonder before we fall to the ground on the level below. We land in the middle of a walk-in freezer. I start shivering as I help Tony to his feet. I find it strange that this freezer still has power going to it. I figured after the fire happened that the power would be gone for good. Especially since the residents are now Reapers to say the least. The fridge itself seems to be spared from fire damage. We walk through the refrigerator doors and out into a large food pantry that was spared as well. I haven't gone this way before, but I still have a good sense of our general location. This must be on the same level as the indoor crop fields.

"You ready to go again?" I ask him.

He smiles. "Let's do this." I can tell he's enjoying Connor's gift.

We start moving through the floor a little faster than I intended this time. We land on top of a storage crate. Tony moves towards the end of the crate to jump down, but he freezes when he reaches the edge. "We have company," he tells me.

I move to his side and peer down over his shoulder. Three of Zack's goons are standing there with their guns pointed towards us. More of his men, dressed in black, are running our way. "Smart move," I say aloud. Zack knew I'd eventually have to come this way so he littered it with men.

"Surrender your weapons," a large man with yellow eyes yells up to us.

Tony looks at me and I give him the look that says we had better cooperate. I hand him my pistol and he pulls his out. Then he removes the magazines from both of them and drops the pistols and the magazines separately to the ground beneath us.

One of the other men grabs the pistols quickly, leaving the magazines on the floor. "Get down here," the man demands.

Tony hops down first. The men don't flinch; they just keep their guns trained on us. Tony holds his arms up to me and I allow myself to drop into them. Even without super-human strength, Tony is built. He catches me with ease and holds me close to him before settling me down on the ground, keeping his arm secured around me, not daring to let go.

"Move," the man says, nudging Tony with his gun.

Surrounded by trigger-happy soldiers, we start walking in the direction of the late Dr. Hastings's lab. We wind down a few hallways and I notice that this area of the shelter was untouched by the fire. I wonder how much of it actually burned. Was it just enough to get everyone to run outside? Was anyone hurt in the fire?

The normally locked doors are wide open, but two armed men guard the entrance. They eye us suspiciously as we walk past. Only a few more steps until I find my family and friends. Will they be okay? My heart leaps in anticipation. They have to be.

"Willow!" Zack says in an overzealous voice. He meets me at the entrance to the lab. His smile grins from ear to ear as he looks me over from head to toe. He seems pleased when he sees that I followed his orders and brought Tony and only Tony with me.

"Zack," I say with as much disgust as I can muster, which is a whole heck of a lot. I try to move past him to see if my family is inside but someone blocks me with a gun to the forehead.

"It's okay, you can let her through," Zack tells the soldier. He puts his hand on the lower part of my back. I try to arch forward to get away from his touch.

At the same time, Tony tries to remove Zack's hand, but someone with too much strength for their own good hits him in the shoulder with the butt of their gun, sending Tony to his knees.

I whip around when the goon tries to hit him again. "Stop!" I yell. Using my mind, I rip the gun out of his hand and throw it behind him. It clips the man on the side of his head on the way down; then it lands with a thud on the concrete floor.

He nurses the wound on his head and shoots me an angry glare.

Zack laughs behind me. "Stop showing off, sugar." He grabs my arm and pulls me forcefully towards the lab. I glance back at Tony before Zack pulls me into the room.

"Sabby! Dad!" I see them first and run to their side. They are sitting on the ground, their hands tied behind their backs. They look dazed as they lean up against the wall. I see Alec, Marya, Connor, and Claire sitting across from them, leaning up against the island counter. Everyone looks drugged and disoriented. At least I don't see the weird collars on their necks. "What did you do to them?" I spin around and point all of my anger at Zack.

He smiles and holds his hands up in the air. "Nothing permanent! Don't worry. I just convinced them to sit very, very still and to shut up. That little Sebastian has a lot to say."

I look back at my little baby brother. I want to strangle Zack for messing with him. "He's just a baby!" I yell at Zack.

"Like I said, I only convinced them. I didn't hurt them...Yet. That's up to you, sugar. You can play by the rules and have a happy ever after... Or you can be difficult." He weighs the options with his hands bent at the elbow next to his sides. He cocks his head and gives me a sidelong look, waiting for my deliberation.

"There is no happy ever after," I say under my breath. If there were, my baby brother and everyone else I love would not be in this room. My mom would not be dead. I look back at Zack and any thoughts of whether it would be wrong to take a life go out the window as I stare into this monster's hazel eyes. "Fine. What do you want, Zack?"

He cocks his eyebrow. "Did you not read my letter?"

I roll my eyes. "Yes, I did. I've told you though that

I don't know how I got these powers."

He advances forward until he's all up in my business. "Yes, and you lied!" I can feel little droplets of spit hit my face as he yells at me, but I don't take a step back. I refuse to show any weakness.

"It won't work anyway, Zack. Your blood is already tainted. You've been immunized. Look, I will turn myself in here and now and you can let my friends and family leave this place safely," I tell him.

He laughs in my face. "Ha! I'm not going to deal with you for the rest of my life. I can be a clean slate too. Just like your precious Tony."

I eye him suspiciously. "Do you seriously want me to try and Reap your powers out of you?" I try to give him my most malicious smile before taking an intimidating step towards him. I find pleasure in the fact that he takes a step back.

"No. You don't think my father created these powers without an antidote to remove them, do you?" He grabs a syringe with clear fluid in it. He looks to one of the men in the room, who is holding a gun. "If she tries to compel me or use any of her other gifts on me, kill them all." Zack turns his attention to me and gives me an, 'I know better than you,' grin.

I roll my eyes. "So there *is* a way to make us all normal again," I say.

He doesn't answer me. Instead, he injects himself with the fluid. He stares at me the whole time, not even looking down as he presses the fluid into his bloodstream.

170

I ready myself to laugh at him because nothing is happening. Then, before my eyes, I watch his hazel eyes fade into a deep, baby blue. He smiles at my astonished expression. "What, did you think it wouldn't work?"

I scoff. "Whatever, let's just get this over with." I look over at Tony. "If you want me to do this, you are going to have to call off your monkeys. I don't want them in on this little trick," I say to Zack.

Zack shakes his finger at me. "You do know that I instructed my people, in a very convincing manor, to kill you and your family the instant you try to take me out. Right?"

I try to look shocked. I don't have to try to look disgusted though; I'm always disgusted when I look at Zack. "Fine, I get your point. No killing you."

He nods his head. "Let's just be double sure that you understand." He turns around to face his men. "Take the boy and the old man!"

"No!" I yell as two large men move forward. I throw myself in front of my family. "Over my dead body!" I say with venom.

The men hesitate. Zack makes an annoyed sound then says, "Fine, *carefully* remove them from the room and take them next door. They are to remain safe as long as this girl and her friend don't try to kill me. Do you understand?" Zack tells the men.

Their eyes don't glaze over. Zack no longer has the use of his compulsion. I think he realizes this at the same moment that I do and he looks to me. "They will still obey me. My first order that I gave them stands and will not be erased from their mind so easily."

I watch with worried eyes as the men move forward. One man gently picks up Sabby. He cradles him like a baby in his huge arms. Sabby looks so small and fragile. The man looks into my eyes. His eyes are black as night. I open myself up to sense his emotions. He's full of conflict but I can tell that he has no intention of harming my brother... Unless he's forced to.

The other man with bright yellow eyes picks up my dad by throwing him over his shoulder as if he weighs nothing. Then the four of them leave the room with the last of my living family. My heart falls. I can't fail in this mission.

The doors close with finality. I stare down at my friends, who are still incapacitated. Then I look at Tony, who is standing behind Zack. He gives me a nod and I watch his hand reaching to his back pocket.

"So what changed your mind? Why do you all of a sudden want me to tell you how I got these powers again?" I try to distract Zack.

"I'm not going to try to chase you down every time you manage to escape my grasp. I need the powers you have. I won't only be the most powerful person in the world, but I can also sell my own blood for crazy money. It's a win-win situation," he says matter-of-factly.

"Then what about us?" I ask. "After I show you this, how do I know that you will just let us go like that?"

He clucks his tongue. "You don't know."

I glare at him. "Then if we are going to die anyway, let it be. I'm not helping you."

"I'll let you go!" Zack says with exasperation.

"And my family and all of my friends?" I clarify.

He rolls his eyes. "Yes, yes of course."

"And you will leave us alone forever?" I ask.

"Yes," he says again, his voice hinting at agitation.

I have no reason to believe him. "This is too much power for someone like you to have," I tell him. "Or anyone to have for that matter."

"I don't care what you think, Willow. You are doing this, and you are doing it now. The sun will only be up for a few more hours and I want this done today." He points at me with each word.

I try not to glance over at Tony because I don't want Zack to turn around. I can sense that he's already moved over to where the injections lie. I pray that he's made the switch. Zack does not want to mess around anymore.

"Are you sure, Zack? You could just let us all go and you could change your ways. You don't have to be like your father. I know you must have a heart somewhere deep down. You don't have to do any of this." I throw him one last lifeline but I already know deep down this is my attempt at stalling. I mean seriously, is he going to say, '*Oh sure, Willow. Let's just call the whole thing off.*'

"Shut up already! I'm getting sick of this tête-à-tête. We are doing this and there is no going back. I deserve to have the power you possess." He points at his chest. "I deserved it from the beginning! Now tell me how you did it!" His face is filled with anger and annoyance.

I gave him a chance to keep his life. He didn't take it. I look behind him at the many needles filled with different colors. There are two different trays. "I was given the dark green shot. Then I took the red shot," I say simply.

Zack eyes me, trying to call my bluff. "You're lying." When I don't budge or flinch, his expression turns to shock. "How did you survive? The only way to survive after taking the red shot is if you've had the survival one first."

I shrug my shoulders. "I don't know. I wasn't the monster who made this crap up."

As usual, Zack is unaffected by any negative talk about his dad. He knows just as well as I do that his dad was horrible. He killed his wife, Zack's mom, over his lust for power. Zack says, "Fine, if that's how you got all of that..." He circles his finger at me. "Then let's test this theory out on your boy. He's the perfect candidate since he's basically a clean slate and all..."

He turns on Tony. Then he picks up the dark green injection and the red one from the tray closest to Tony. My heart races. *Did he switch it out? Is that the right red shot? There are two different ones. Surely, Tony would have switched out the needle closest to him. I hope.* All of those questions and thoughts run rampant in my mind. I wish I could talk to Tony in the way we used to, in our private way. "Let me do it!" I yell at Zack when he moves towards Tony.

Zack spins around and eyes me suspiciously. Then he shrugs his shoulders. "Fine, whatever." He places the two shots on the counter.

I walk to Tony and stand in front of him. "I love you," I whisper to him as I pick up the green immunization. He smiles lovingly at me. "I love you always." He holds out his arm for me.

Zack makes a mock gagging sound behind us. "Just get on with it."

I shoot him the stink eye and then I take Tony's arm. I slowly inject the dark green liquid into Tony's vein. My heart is accelerating at unnatural speeds as I empty the entire syringe into his arm. I pray that this will work. There is too much at risk. *Could he die because of this?* I think to myself as I pick up the next needle. The thick, bright red liquid looks off. I can only hope that it's the right one. Surely Tony wouldn't accept it if he didn't make the switch. Even still, I cringe as I bring it up to Tony's arm. "I love you," I tell him again before I empty the contents into his bloodstream.

We stare into each other's eyes for what seems like an eternity. I search for any sign of something going wrong. Nothing, no sign.

Zack starts laughing giddily. "He didn't die!" he says gleefully, clapping his hands. "This is it!" He seems way too excited. He laughs again, evilly, maniacally. "Let's go outside and test this out!" he says. I look at him because he's so overexcited that it is sickening. He grabs the two shots from the other tray. Then he grabs a remote control device. I recognize it as the one that keeps the Reapers incapacitated. He walks towards the door, waving his hand over his head, "Let's get moving."

Tony grabs my hand and we follow behind Zack. He leads us down a few hallways until we reach a stairwell. A few guards are following closely behind Tony and me, making sure we stay in line.

We walk up two flights of stairs until we reach a long hallway. We walk down another hallway that leads us to the commons area. Zack laughs at the Reapers who are still crying on the ground. Instead of walking around the Reapers, he steps on them like they are stepping-stones. Zack has gone mad. He keeps laughing and laughing like he's enjoying his own private joke.

We follow him all the way outside. When we walk out into the sun, Zack turns around abruptly and watches Tony like he's the most amazing sight he's ever seen.

I turn to look at Tony. The snow clouds have drifted away from the sun, whose rays are shining strong overhead. The air is cold but the sunrays provide their own glow of warmth amidst the chilly air. I hold Tony's hand and we stare into each other's eyes. I have no idea if this will work. It's merely the theory I had. The only guess I could come up with as to why I was special. His eyes turn from brown to a dark hunter green. I smile when I see the new color. A few more minutes pass, then a red speck shows up near both of his pupils. My heart starts hammering. *Please let him be okay, please let him be okay.* I repeat the mantra over and over again in my head.

"I *will* be okay." He smiles and reaches his hand up to my cheek. Hope fills me. He heard my thoughts. I can't help the smile that takes over my face.

I look at him in amazement as the colors begin swimming in. Navy, purple, brown, hazel, light blue, neon yellow, black, copper, silver, gold, and a small swirl of white. My eyes widen as the colors do a tornado dance around his irises. Tony squeezes my hand. I still can't believe it worked and that I'm not alone.

Zack's horrible laugh cuts into this intimate moment between Tony and me. When Tony's eyes look at Zack, I turn to look too. Zack is already injecting himself with the green shot.

"Stop!" I yell at Zack.

"Never," he says with a snarky expression. He looks behind us at his men. They point their guns at our backs. "Don't even try to stop me," he says.

"You don't want to do this," I tell him again.

"Shut up, Willow. When I'm more powerful than you are, I will end you, sugar. You are so stupid. You thought I'd let you go!" He laughs hysterically.

I watch in horror as he lifts the red shot up to his arm. Everything happens in slow motion. The needle enters his skin. Then he starts emptying the red liquid into his veins. He looks so power hungry and excited as he imagines his future filled with power, a future that will never happen.

He pulls the needle out of his vein and drops the emptied shot onto the ground. It lands on the snow with a small thud. A small drop of blood is forming at the injection site. Zack stumbles forward as Tony and I take a step backwards. The soldiers step back with us. Zack's face goes from overly excited, to realization, to fear. He tries to take another step forward but he falls to his knees. Looking up at me, he opens his mouth, but nothing comes out. He reaches forward with his hand and then falls face forward into the snow.

The soldiers don't try to move forward to check on him. Instead, they seem confused as to what they should do now. Tony turns around slowly to look at the men with the guns. "put your guns down. he killed himself. we did not kill him. you are free of his charge."

I watch them put their guns down on the ground. I look at Tony, whose eyes are hazel. I would smile, but the whole situation is too sickening to warrant any upturn of my lips.

I move back over to where Zack is lying face down on the ground. I grab the control device from his hand and stand up to look at the largest of the soldiers. I tell him. "Go find all of the other soldiers. tell them to leave now. tell them to go to their homes, to find their families. they are not to fight anymore."

The soldier's eyes glaze over and he nods his head. He tells the man next to him to go home before he walks back into the den of Reapers. Tony and I run past him, back towards Dr. Hastings's lab. I don't have to hold Tony's hand to move through the floor. He moves through just as easily as I do. Tony smiles at me with brown eyes when we land on the level below us. I smile back and we move down one more level. Dropping on top of another storage container, we both hop down with ease and run towards the lab. Tony keeps pace with me easily. When we reach the lab, Tony uses his compulsion to call off the last of the soldiers that Zack had compelled.

I stand amazed at Tony, watching him use his powers, knowing how long it took me to get a handle on my own. This is his first run using them and he already looks like an expert. A satisfied feeling comes over media know that Tony will keep his head out of the clouds despite his increased ability to do just about anything. It's easy to let all of this power go to your head.

We burst through the door of the lab and find our friends right where we left them. We rush over to them and begin untying them.

"My dad and Sabby..." I say to Tony.

"They'll be fine. Let's get these four and then we'll go find them," he assures me.

I nod in understanding, even though my stomach disagrees. The desire to find my dad and Sebastian is so great that it takes all I am to stay here and work on untying my friends.

After a few minutes of struggle, we have everyone free. Alec, Connor, Marya, and Claire look around the room, still dazed. I squat down to their level and look them in the eyes. "You guys, I need you to fight whatever it is in your systems..." Then I smack my forehead. My brain isn't working at full capacity right now. Not with my desire to find my family. "Tony, help me heal them."

He gives me a look that says, 'why didn't I think of that," and his eyes turn a deep navy blue.

"Make sure you're careful not to exert yourself," I remind Tony after remembering how many times I passed out when I was first getting used to my powers. He gives me a small nod as we watch everyone come to...

Claire's eyes focus on me first. She wraps her arms around me and squeezes. I hug her back, but end it just as quickly. "I'm so glad you're okay, Claire Bear, but we need to go find my dad and Sebastian," I say. She nods her head in affirmation and immediately gets to her feet. She's all business now.

Alec, Connor, Marya, and Tony are on their feet. Tony takes the lead. I call out to my dad and Sabby, even though I'm pretty sure they can't respond. There are multiple doors next to the lab and, together, we search them one at a time. My heart lurches in my chest each time we find an empty room. We could cover more space if we separated, but I don't think anyone wants that right now.

I open the door to the third room and I exhale a loud breath of relief. Both my dad and Sabby are huddled together on the cold tile floor. "Dad...Sabby." I kneel before them and Tony and I wiggle them out of their restraints.

Alec comes over and helps us heal them. I watch the light slowly come back into their eyes. When Sabby's lips puff out and he jumps into my arms, my heart leaps in my chest.

"I was berry brave, Wello," he tells me. His eyes still look scared though. "Just like you tol me."

"I know, Sabby. You are so brave," I tell him. I hold him tightly while getting to my feet. Cradling his head in my hands, relief pours over me. My dad joins in the embrace and for just a moment, the whole world feels right. I reluctantly let go of my family and set Sabby down at my side. He hops into our dad's arms, who gratefully scoops him up. His copper eyes are shining with tears as he looks from Sabby to me.

I take a deep breath and turn to Tony. "Tony, would you stay in the front and take the lead? I'm going to remain in the back and make sure everyone gets out safely."

He nods and turns towards the door. As soon as it's open, we all fall into line as Tony leads us into the hall. We take the same path we took before, when Zack was leading us outdoors.

We make it up the two flights of stairs. Tony pauses at the entrance to the commons area. Even though I know that the Reapers are incapacitated, I can't help but feel like there is still danger lurking around every corner in this burnt shell of a shelter. Up ahead, I see my dad tug Sebastian's little head against his chest, blocking his eyes from this horrifying sight. Sabby holds his little hands over his ears, trying to block out the cries.

Claire stops and gags from the smell that the fire left behind. I put my hand on her back and try to encourage her to keep moving. Connor has stopped to help her too, but the others have already made it to the tunnel that leads outside. I don't like them being so far ahead of us.

"Shallow breaths, Claire. Don't breathe through your mouth," I tell her from experience.

Connor strokes her hair a few times and then puts

his arm around her back to help her keep moving.

When we make it to the tunnel, the others are already out of sight. They must have gone straight outside.

A gunshot rings out from somewhere in front of us and I panic. The sound was close… too close. My ears ring uncomfortably and I push Claire and Connor aside. I move with all my might to get to where Tony is. I have to make sure he's okay. I reach the exit and the sunlight momentarily blinds me. Another gunshot rings out, followed by a scream. It's a guttural cry and immediately I can tell it came from my dad.

"Dad!" the title I've always called him, rings from my lips. "Sebastian!" I look to the left to see Zack lying *almost* lifeless on the ground in a pool of his own blood. An eerie smile splays on his lips and he raises his gun and points it at me.

I watch in slow motion as his index finger pulls back on the trigger. I swear I see the bullet that's coming towards my head, but then it's gone! Zack's eyes widen in surprise and the gun is flung from his hand.

I turn to see where the gun was magically thrown to and I see Marya grab it out of the air. Her eyes are molten gold as she looks from Zack to me. I realize in that moment that she just saved my life. Our joke about her being able to stop a bullet with her mind was no joke at all. She just pushed the bullet off its course and saved me. I mouth the words, "thank you," to her.

She nods her head and then focuses her golden eyes on Zack. Her utter disdain for him is obvious. She trains the gun on him to make sure he doesn't move.

I rush over to my dad. Tony and my dad are crowded around someone…a pool of blood around their feet. Everything happens so fast that I can't get my mind to wrap around what's going on. We're supposed to be safe!

I hear sobs coming from my dad. I'm afraid to look and then I realize what's going on. It's not my dad that's hurt, it's Sebastian. "No, no, no!" I cry as the sickening reality sets in.

I fall to the ground at my dad's feet and can't even concentrate. It's like my own mind is trying to protect me from what's happening. My father's shoulder moves just enough to reveal Sebastian lying lifeless before media scream aloud and crawl to where he is, ignoring the blood that soaks into my pants and stains my hands. I place my palms on him, along with Alec and Tony, who have already started working on him. I try to focus on healing him, but can't stop crying. Sobs bellow from deep within media feel Claire's presence as she sits down at my side. She places her hand on my back, not sure what else to do. I can hear her softly crying. Sebastian coughs and more blood sprays from his mouth. Tony removes a bullet from Sebastian's little body and I dry heave, not able to handle the sight. I put my head down, making sure I keep my hand on Sebastian, exerting every ounce of strength I have on healing him.

Alec begins to sit Sebastian up and I watch as the blood flow begins slowing, clotting up as the wound begins to disappear. His eyes flutter open and I watch the life come back in his face. His neon-yellow eyes remind me of mom's. It's in that moment that I realize Sebastian's going to live to see another day. It's also the moment that I decide that someone else won't get that opportunity.

"You Bastard!" I scream at the top of my lungs. I let go of Sebastian and rise to my feet. The anger pours out of me, every cell in my being is on fire. Zack lies on the ground, staring up at me with his sick, twisted expression. I take the gun from Marya. You!" I scream, pointing the gun at him. "I thought you were dead! You're nothing but an oxygen whore. You don't deserve the three seconds I'm going to give you to live, before I pull this trigger and end your life for good."

I watch his eyes roll back in his head for a second before he looks back at me. There's a red hurricane swirling around his irises. A small amount of green is still left, but I can see death knocking at his door. I think back to what the nurse had told me the red shot does, an instant, swift, painless death. It doesn't look like she was right and for that I'm grateful. This dirt bag deserves none of those things.

He isn't all the way gone, but he's close. He's fighting death; it's only a matter of time. But I want him to suffer! Just like he's made me suffer...and my mother... and Tony...and almost everyone near and dear to my heart. "You've taken everything I love at one time or another, and now, you will pay." I drop the gun at my feet.

Zack studies me, obviously he expected me to shoot him. That would have been the easy way out. I look back over to Sebastian and although the tears still fall from my eyes, I can't help but give him a smile as he continues to heal. *This is for you, baby.*

Tony's stands up, only Alec remains on the ground helping Sabby.

I address everyone through clenched teeth. "I need to take care of something. If you will all meet us at the tree line, we'll be right back."

No one dares say anything. They can see the anger permeating from the core of my being. My eyes fight to go red, but I won't let them. I can't lose control in a time like this. I eye Tony and he comes to my side. "Help me get him back to the commons."

He nods his head once, picks up Zack, and slings him over his shoulder. Zack lets out a grunt as more blood drips from his mouth. I take the lead this time, leading them into the shelter. We enter into the mountain and walk through the tunnel. I glance over at Tony and grit my teeth at Zack. Revenge has run its course. It's my turn now. I have much to avenge for.

When we reach the commons area filled with Reapers writhing in pain, I find a chair in the corner and step over the Reapers, who still moan beneath my feet. I grab the chair and resituate it in the middle of the room. I hear Zack cough as Tony throws him onto the chair. Grabbing a belt from one of the Reaper's pants, I use it to secure Zack in the chair.

Realization dawns on Zack and a look of panic flashes in his eyes.

I stare at him for a moment more. No words are said between us, it's not needed. I will finally win and I'll win for good. "Do you still have the remote?" I ask Tony, even though I know the answer. I saw the antenna poking out of his pocket on the way over here. He gives me a nod anyway, takes it out of his pocket, and shows it in plain sight.

I turn away from Zack and take Tony's hand as we walk towards the exit. Right before we get to the tunnel, I stop and look at Tony. He tries to hand me the remote but I shake my head. "I can't," I say. As angry as I am, I can't bring myself to press that button alone.

Tony takes my hand in his and then places our fingers over the button together. "On three," he says to me. "One...two...three." We both push the button and the high-pitch tone silences. I look into Tony's purple eyes. We are both invisible. We stand there for a few moments as we watch the Reapers come to. They seem to all stand at once. Immediately, they recognize Zack and that's all I need to see.

Tony and I run down the narrow tunnel into the light outside. Screams from Zack bounce off the walls, which only calm me as we walk out into the light of day. This is finally over. When we can hear him no more, Tony switches the button back on. The last thing we need is for them to come after us next.

My friends and family stand amongst the trees. My father holds Sebastian. They're still covered in blood, as am I, but we don't care. We are only relieved to see him alive. I rush over to him and take Sabby into my arms. I give him the once over, making sure he's okay.

"Wello," he says. "Sank you for saving me," he tells me as he hugs me close.

I close my eyes and relish his hug. "I will always be there for you, Sabby. Always," I say, even though I know it may not be the truth. This life is fragile and it can break with the flick of a finger. I give him a kiss on the top of his head and hand him back to my dad.

It will take all of us a long time to get over this, to forget the image of my brother bleeding out in that clearing. An icy breeze ruffles Sabby's curls and he tucks his head into my dad's shoulder. My dad looks to me. "I am so proud of you, Willow." His copper eyes are filled to the brim with emotion. "You definitely take after your mother." His smile isn't sad; it's filled with a fond memory.

"Thanks, Dad." I smile back.

I hear Sabby giggling in my father's arms. I turn to see what has captured his attention. Connor is acting like he's walking up and down stairs, which in and of itself wouldn't usually capture a laugh from anyone other than a four-year-old, but the fact that he is using his ability to sink half of his body underground is quite noteworthy. Sabby's little laughter keeps Connor, who always uses comedic relief to ease tensions, motivated. He drops into the ground all the way until all you can see are his head and arms sticking out of the snow, and then he pretends to swim in the white ocean. That gains a snort from my little brother, who's laughing hysterically now. When Connor gets pelted in the back of the head with a snowball, all of us join in with the contagious laughter. Connor turns his head to see Alec trying to hide behind a tree. He doesn't make it before a snowball smacks him in the butt, complements of Connor, who has emerged from the white ocean. His clothes are covered with snow, making him look like a marshmallow. I watch as Claire runs and jumps on his back, tackling him back down in the snow. She's small, but with her invisibility, she has the element of surprise on her side.

Something inside me warms up at this sight. Things seem to be turning around for the better again. I allow myself to hope, something I once thought would never be possible. I see Tony and Marya standing at opposite sides of the ongoing snow fight. I smile at Tony, raise my finger asking for a moment, and then I walk over to Marya.

She notices me approaching and shuffles a little from side to side nervously. I try to give her a warm smile so she knows I'm not coming to start drama.

"Hey, Marya," I say. From the corner of my eye, I can see Alec staring at us with a worried expression. He gives us our space though.

"Hey." Her voice is quiet. Her golden eyes look haunted. I never stopped to think about just how much this life has affected her. I wonder what kind of woman Marya would have become if ELE never came along. What kind of woman would I have become?

"I want to thank you again, Marya," I say. Her eyes widen in surprise. "You saved my life today. You stopped a bullet for me and you didn't have to."

She cocks her head to the side. "Of course I did. I would never willingly let anyone hurt you or anyone for that matter," she says.

I nod my head. "I know that. I guess what I meant was that I know I haven't been exactly..." I search for the words, "...welcoming." I bite my lip and swallow my pride, my Achilles heel.

Her lips twitch up slightly as she watches me.

I continue, "I'm sorry about that and I would like us to be friends. I can see that Alec really likes you and he has impeccable taste so you must be a pretty awesome girl." Her lips give another slight twitch as I get her to smile. It's as though a veil's been lifted and I'm finally able to see her in a different, non-judgmental light.

"Thanks, Willow. I would like that. Alec has said nothing but good things about you. To be honest, it's a little intimidating." She adds a quiet, "I've got some big shoes to fill."

I shake my head. "No, you don't. You are a totally different person and that's a good thing. I'm not sure how to explain this but, for example, when I'm with Tony, I don't measure him up to Alec. I don't even think about Alec and me in that way or judge how the two are different. That's because Tony didn't replace Alec. I fell in love with Tony for who he is. I'm sure it's the same for Alec and you..." I realize that I just made the mention of Alec possibly loving Marya. What surprises me is that the thought doesn't hurt. In fact, it pleases me. I want Alec to be happy. I want him to feel complete. I finish up with, "Please don't be intimidated by me or mine and Alec's friendship. We really are just friends now. I love Tony so much that it hurts. I hope that you can do the same for Alec. He deserves happiness."

Her eyes lighten up and she nods her head. She looks from me to Alec, who is still watching us from afar, but not close enough to hear our conversation. "Thanks, Willow. That means a lot to me. I know what it's like to lose someone you love. I'm glad you were able to get Tony back."

I smile and look back at Tony, who's staring at me with ready eyes. "Me too." I hold my hand out to Marya. She laughs as we both shake on it. "Friends," I say.

"Friends." She smiles.

I waste no time turning around and running into Tony's arms. He grabs me and lifts me up. His strength is back. I look into his multicolored eyes that now match mine. We are together again, no doom and gloom hanging over our shoulders. I take a deep breath and try to allow myself to take this moment in. We are safe, we are together, things are right again.

Tony tucks a strand of hair behind my ear. He leans his forehead against mine and takes a deep breath. "Whoa," he says. "I can feel..." He leans back and looks into my eyes. "...what you are feeling." His eyes reflect black ebony.

My heart flutters as he looks at me with that unadulterated love. I open myself up to feel the emotions that soar from his heart: thankfulness, gratefulness, a small mix of worry about the future, but mostly love. I move up on my tiptoes and kiss him gently on the lips.

My dad clears his throat, which prompts us to end our PDA. My cheeks heat as I look up at Tony and give an embarrassed laugh. "Sorry, Dad."

"Mmhmm," he says but I can tell he isn't annoyed. He's just happy we are all alive and well, at least for the moment.

I look up to see that the sun is setting in the sky and the moon is beginning to rise. A cold wind blows around us, making me uncomfortable. Tony takes his jacket off and places it over my shoulders. He puts his arms around me and I lean into him. "I love you," I whisper to him.

"I love you too," he says in my thoughts. I hadn't thought we'd ever get that gift back but it only makes sense. We are the same now. I give him a smile of relief, thankful Zack is officially out of the picture. There's no chance he'll come back to haunt us now. The finalization of his death gives me a peace I didn't know I could possess.

"Is everyone ready to head back?" I ask the group.

The cold has really sunk in, so everyone gives me a shivery yes. We turn to make the long journey back to the camp. The winds are blustery and cold. I shiver, even with the warmth of Tony's jacket around me.

I notice a glowing light in the distance when we are only a little ways away from the camp. "S'mores," I say to Tony excitedly. Memories of bonfires play in my mind. My stomach growls at the mere mention of food.

Tony notices the light as well, and looks at me questioningly. "Do they usually do bonfires at this camp?"

I scrunch my eyebrows. "Maybe they are doing it because Lee and our people are here..." He's right though, something doesn't add up. I stayed in Erik's camp for a long time and never saw them so much as light a fire outside. There are too many Reapers in this area and Erik doesn't like to draw any attention to his safe haven. A strange sensation flutters around in my stomach.

"I don't have a good feeling about this," Tony says as he comes to a halt. We are now only a short distance from the camp. We all stop with him.

"What's going on?" my dad asks.

"I don't know, something feels wrong. It feels off," Tony answers my dad.

All of us huddle around in a circle. Connor beams his flashlight at us. "I feel something strange as well," he says seriously, which is strange since he is rarely serious. He shifts the flashlight around in his hands and the light glances off Sabby's face. My little brother's eyes are sleepy and...

"Wait," I say to Connor. He stops shifting around and looks at me. I grab the flashlight from his hands without asking and shine it in my brother's eyes.

Sabby squints. "Wello!" He covers his blue eyes with his little hands.

"His eyes are blue," Tony says, catching onto what I'm just noticing.

I shine the light on Alec's eyes. "Green," I say. I move it to Claire and notice her light blue eyes, then Connor's black eyes. My dad's eyes match my brother's. Marya's eyes aren't gold, they are hazel. Lastly, Tony's eyes are brown. "What the heck?" I ask.

Tony grabs the flashlight from me and shines it into

my eyes. "I've never seen your original eye color. They're beautiful." We are caught in a strangely intimate moment in front of everyone.

My dad clears his throat, ending the moment. I look over at him. Sabby has already fallen back asleep on his shoulder.

"How?" Alec asks, looking at me.

Connor still isn't getting it, "What's going on? You all are making absolutely no sense at all."

Claire answers her boyfriend. "Everyone's eyes are back to their original color." Tony shines the light in her face and she points to her eyes.

"Oh," Connor says confused.

"I can't move anything with my mind," Marya chimes in. "My powers aren't working."

I try to open my mind to listen to their thoughts but I hear nothing but deafening silence. I run through my other powers, invisibility, moving through objects, nothing is working.

"Maybe the immunizations only lasted so long," My dad says. He clutches my little brother closer to his chest. I can see the unease in his eyes. He cancels his own thought out. "No, that wouldn't make sense. We weren't all injected at the same time. There's something else going on here."

"I have a bad feeling about this," Alec says.

I look to Tony and I don't have to read minds to know that he concurs with Alec. I look back in the direction of the camp. "We should get back there now. They may need help."

Tony grabs my hand and together we lead everyone forward, towards the camp. The closer we get, the more uneasy we feel. Soon we start hearing a muffled voice up ahead, it sounds like it's coming from a microphone or megaphone. We can't make out what is being said but it seems to be the same two phrases being repeated over and over again every minute or so. The lights are more noticeable now that we are only a few yards from the road that leads to the camp entrance. The glow they emit is more white than yellow, which tells us that the light isn't coming from a fire.

Tony stops our group. "This definitely isn't right. There's no electricity out here so there shouldn't be lights like that." He points towards the camp. "I think we need to proceed with caution." He looks to my dad, Alec, and Connor. "Why don't us guys go check out what's happening first?"

"I'm going with you," I tell Tony.

He looks at me. "Have your powers come back?"

I shake my head.

"Then I think you should stay. We'll only go up ahead and take a peek, that's all." When I glare at him, he puts his hands on my shoulders and looks into my eyes. "Please, babe?"

I don't like the idea of not being involved, but I have to remind myself that the world doesn't revolve around Willow. Plus, I find myself feeling a bit insecure without my powers. I've learned to rely on them far too much in the past few months. "Okay. If you aren't back in twenty minutes, I'm coming after you," I tell him.

He kisses me on the cheek. "Love you."

"Love you too."

He smiles at me before he turns around. "Let's go." He waves the guys out.

My dad hands a sleeping Sebastian to me. I didn't realize how heavy my brother is without my super strength. I pull him to me and smile worriedly at my dad. "I love you, Dad."

"I love you too, honey. We'll be right back. Stay hidden please." He looks more alive than he has in a long time. I can imagine that having a daughter who's stronger than him could have been a bit emasculating. I think he likes the idea of taking care of me. There are a lot of things I haven't thought much of lately and involving my dad more in the future is a must.

I watch them walk towards the camp. Marya, Claire, Sebastian, and I move back behind a grouping of large trees. I sit down, since Sabby is getting heavy, and rearrange him on my lap. We continue to listen to the strange voice on the loud speaker that we can't quite make out. My stomach is a ball of nerves.

"What's that?" Claire whispers.

I strain my ear to hear what she's talking about. Marya moves closer to us. Her back is rigid with tension. The sound grows closer and I realize it's the sound of gravel crunching underneath tires. I place my hand to my lips and grip Sabby closer to me. I'm so grateful that he's sleeping. Claire and Marya move as close to us as possible. I hope that the huge trunk of the tree provides adequate cover for us.

I peek around the trunk as best as I can and see a black SUV approaching slowly; it can't be going more than ten miles an hour. I find myself wishing for the cloak our invisibility would have allowed us. Why aren't our powers working? That seems to be the million-dollar question. The SUV stops every few feet and someone inside the vehicle shines a search light out into the woods. The windows are open and the person holds the light out the window as far as they can.

As they approach, I can hear static and voices coming over a handheld radio.

I duck my head back since the SUV is nearly on us. The girls scoot in even closer to me. My heart starts beating heavily in my chest. Sabby stirs, but I rub his back gently, trying to urge him to go back to sleep. I have no idea what's going on. All I can hope is that the guys haven't been spotted. I don't trust anyone who has a vehicle in a time like this.

I hold my breath when I see the light shining on a tree next to us. It moves around and I shift Sabby closer to me when it reflects off the snow on the ground beside us. *Please don't let them see us*, I say over and over again in my head.

With them this close, I can make out the sound of the radio even better. I listen as someone talks into it. The truck is placed in park right next to where we sit, giving us a clear opportunity to hear what's going on. It still sets me at extreme unease having it be this close to us.

"Base command, this is two-one-bravo over," a man's voice calls from the vehicle.

"Go ahead two-one-bravo, this is base command, over," a voice responds back from the radio.

"Base command, two-one-bravo reporting operation: Perimeter is secure," the man says.

"Confirmed two-one-bravo, perimeter secure. SITREP on Whisky Mike? Over," the person on the radio squawks.

"Base command, two-one-bravo reporting negative on Whisky Mike, please advise, over?" The vehicle starts moving again slowly. I see the light hit a tree a few rows down. The voices are getting harder to make out.

"Two-one-bravo, maintain perimeter until we transport occupants to Foxtrot-Oscar-Bravo, over."

"Base command, copy, out," the man in the vehicle says.

The vehicle keeps moving ahead slowly. I can't hear if there is any more to the radio conversation because they are now completely out of my hearing range. I let out the breath I'd been holding. "What in the world is going on here?" I say aloud.

"I don't know," Claire says a little shakily.

Marya looks really nervous. "I grew up on a military base. This isn't good. It sounds like they are taking someone or everyone to the forward operating base. That's what Foxtrot-Oscar-Bravo means."

My heart starts pounding double time. "Do you

think they found the guys?"

Marya shakes her head. "No, they referred to the people they have as occupants. I can only assume they mean the people at the camp... That they're taking them to the base."

"Why would they do that?" Claire asks, her blue eyes wide as saucers.

"I have no idea." Marya shakes her head. She looks at me with a worried look. "They're looking for someone specific though and it sounds like they still haven't found them."

"What do you mean?" I ask, not liking the way she's looking at me.

"He called for a SITREP on Whiskey Mike. That stands for a situation report and Whiskey Mike would be the initials W.M."

I gasp. Willow Mosby. "They are looking for me," I say quietly.

ELEVEN

I sit there stunned by this new revelation.

Claire puts her hand on my knee and tenses up. Her eyes are wide. "Do you hear that?"

My muscles tense and I pull Sabby closer into me. That's when I hear the sound of vehicles approaching.

Marya leans out of view for a second to look around the tree. "Vehicles, lots of them!" she whispers frantically.

We huddle together as they approach. Their headlights light up the forest around us. Truck after truck zooms past us along the road. Unlike the SUV, these trucks aren't looking for anyone. They are headed out. Memories of my parents and Tony being shot and taken away not too long ago, send my mind into a panic. I count the vehicles as they pass, twenty-one in all. I cringe at the odd number. *Please let the guys be safe!*

After the last vehicle passes, we finally allow ourselves to breathe. None of us knows what's going on but all we can hope is that whatever threat was here is gone now.

We wait for a while in silence, hoping the guys will return soon. Sabby stirs beneath me, resituating himself. A rustling in the trees sets me on edge. I look at Claire and Marya and they return my gaze. Nobody dares move or breathe out of fear of the unknown.

Sabby's head bobs up and he looks around. "Daddy?" he questions aloud. I hold my finger to my lips and shake my head. He squints his eyes at me. "What's wong, Wello?"

I grit my teeth and put my finger to his lips, desperate for him to stop talking. I hug him to my chest and the rustling continues, getting closer and closer still.

When a man emerges from the bushes, I almost lose it and scream… until I see that the man is my father. He kneels down and takes Sabby from my arms. My heart is still pounding in my chest as Connor, Alec, and then Tony, joins us.

The sound that had been resonating around us suddenly goes silent. We wait for several long seconds before my dad breaks the silence.

"We think they're gone. "All three of us girls breathe a sigh of relief. I let my head go back and rest itself on the tree trunk behind me. Tony takes my hands, pulls me to my feet, and into a hug. His comfort and warmth makes me feel safe. He strokes my head as my dad gives a full report.

"We saw several vehicles down on the other side of the camp loading in all of Lee and Eric's people. They seemed to be going willingly. We assume it was because they had no abilities to use to defend themselves. Eric and Lee were the last to get loaded into the trucks. They're the only ones who looked as if they'd been in a scuffle. No doubt, they didn't go down without a fight. As to where they're going…that we aren't sure of. We overheard some talk on the walkie-talkies but couldn't make out what they were saying."

"Marya can," I say, almost cutting off my dad. "Marya's dad was military. She heard what they said and told us what it meant."

My dad looks impressed. "Well…what did they say?" he asks, almost losing his composure. I can tell he's irritated and on the verge of panic. He desperately wants all the puzzle pieces so he can fit them together.

"They're looking for Willow," Marya says quietly.

The look in my dad's eyes is fierce as understanding flashes before him. "Impossible," I hear my dad whisper.

"They're taking all of the people they gathered to a nearby base, probably less than twenty-five miles from here based on what they said. That's all I really know. I'm sorry I can't be of more help. "Her voice becomes quiet as Alec comforts her.

I swallow hard, realizing the situation seems to be going down the toilet. *So much for peace, harmony, or happily ever after*, I think to myself.

"Tell me about it," I hear a voice say in my head. I look up to Tony and shine my flashlight on his face. I see his eyes have changed back to the wide array of colors they were before.

"Powers," I say aloud. "Our powers are back." I look at the others around me. Their eyes changed back to the colors that correspond to their gifts. I watch as they each test their abilities and come away with satisfied smiles.

"Why they looking for Wello?" Sabby asks as if he just clued in to that detail.

Tony smiles at Sabby. "Because your sister is a very special girl."

My little brother nods his head, his bright yellow eyes showing adoration for me.

Snow starts falling again. Unlike the last time, this moment isn't exactly filled with excitement. The night is cold and the events that have unfolded within it leave us feeling shaken and scared. "We should find shelter," I say.

"The camp isn't safe anymore. They may have left a few of their troops behind to see if you show up. Let's go back to the cabin," Tony suggests.

"That's not exactly a safe place. We were abducted from there, you remember?" Connor adds.

"Yes, but that was Zack's men. I don't think what's going on here is part of his operation," Tony says. "This was a military takeover."

"Still, it might not be secure," Alec agrees with Connor.

"Maybe we should go to the other safe house. Where our people went. You said that Lee came here to inform you when Sebastian and I were taken, but I doubt he would have brought everyone along. Did he?" my dad asks me.

I shake my head. "No, he only had a group of no more than twenty people." A memory comes moving into the forefront of my mind. "Lee had said that they found a way to make contact with the Department of Defense. Do you think that could be what prompted this military takeover?"

My dad considers it for a moment. "It could very well be. It wouldn't explain why they would be looking for you though."

"It doesn't," I say. A small inkling of hope fills me. Perhaps they aren't looking for me. The initials W.M. could stand for a lot of things. What things? I don't know, but I'm sure if I think on it for a little while, they will come to mind.

"*It could stand for whacko-maniac. Or woman-man. Maybe Wal-Mart?*" Tony says inside my head.

"*Listening in, huh?*" I raise my brow at him.

"*I can't help it; your voice is like a siren's song.*" He wags his eyebrows back at me.

"Suck up," I say aloud. My dad looks between the two of us. I quickly get back to the subject at hand. "Do you know how to get back to the safe house?" I ask my dad.

He nods his head. "I believe so, but it's a long way from here. It could take half a day."

"Then it's settled. We will go back to the cabin to take shelter tonight. Then tomorrow at first light, we will try to meet up with the others," Tony says.

I try my best not to shiver when I nod my head to agree. "Let's get moving. I don't like being out here."

When we arrive at the cabin, everyone is exhausted and cold. Tony and I perform a perimeter search and see no signs of any danger in the immediate area. We rush inside and Tony begins making a fire to warm the living room. I grab all of the blankets and coats I can find and we make a large pallet on the floor near the fire.

My dad tucks a large, down jacket around my sleeping brother. He lies down at his side and looks up at me where I lie on the sofa. "What I don't get is why I didn't see any of this coming." My dad seems lost in thought.

I've been thinking the same thing. "I know. I would have assumed that between the two of us, we would have at least had an inkling of what was about to happen. I got nothing."

"I know," my dad says.

Tony comes over and makes a spot for himself on the floor, directly below where I lie on the sofa. He pulls the Sherpa blanket up over my shoulders before he lies his head down on a sofa pillow. "My guess is that it has something to do with the fact that we lost our powers. Something caused our powers to turn off back there. I don't know what it was, but it had to do with the military being there because when they left, we powered up again. That's not a coincidence," he says.

"Yeah, that was some freaky crud. Heck, these past few months have been filled with nothing but Twilight Zone-worthy events," Connor chimes in. He's lying between Claire and Alec on the floor.

"Dude, stop trying to play footsies with me." Alec scoots further away from Connor.

"Sorry, man." Connor laughs. "I couldn't help myself."

Alec groans. I can tell he's tired. Marya lies next to him, closest to the fire. Her eyelids are fluttering heavily as she tries to stay awake.

"Boys," My dad chides and Connor and Alec quiet down.

"What do you think they are going to do with everyone?" Claire asks in a worried whisper.

"I don't know," I say thinking of Erik, Morgan, Audrey, Molly, Candy, Jake, Lee, and all of the people who have helped me survive out here. "We will find a way to help them though," I say with confidence. That's what this life is about now. It's all about trying to survive on the outside and helping others when you can. Everyone agrees with me sleepily.

I stare into the fire for what seems like hours, while everyone else falls asleep. I'm physically exhausted but I can't bring myself to shut my eyes. I wait until I hear the soft sounds coming from everyone sleeping. I gently shake Tony and watch his eyes flutter open. "Tony," I whisper.

He gives me one of his spicy smiles and I nearly melt. "I want to try something. "His eyes perk up and I quickly realize how he must have taken that. I slap his arm playfully. "You are such a goof."

He closes his eyes and gives his head a playful shake. "You're killing me, Willow," he says impishly.

"No really," I try again, ignoring his playfulness. "I can't sleep."

"I'm sorry, babe." He reaches his hand up and rubs my shoulder. "Is there anything you need? I could compel you to sleep if you want." He gives me a half smile.

"Actually, I've been lying here thinking about a gift that neither of us has used yet."

He furrows his brows, trying to connect the dots. "Which one would that be?"

"It's a bit hard to explain but if you would let me, I'd like to try it out with you."

"A bit vague I see, but I'm always up for spending time with you, Willow. There isn't anyone I'd rather spend my sleepless nights with." He sits up and places his hand on my cheek.

"I agree completely." I place my hand over his.

I can tell what I just said means a lot to Tony. His eyes bore into mine in that bad boy sort of way that makes me crazy about him. He looks around us, making sure everyone's asleep, and then helps me to my feet. He grabs a candle and lights it, using the fireplace. Then we creep upstairs so no one will be able to hear us. It's noticeably colder up here with the absence of heat. I shiver and he puts his arm around me.

"So, are you going to tell me what this new gift is?" He pulls me closer to him. We take a seat on his bed.

I wish I had brought a blanket up with us, since we stripped all of the bedding from his bed to make the pallets downstairs.

"I'll get you a sweater," Tony says, reading my mind. He jumps up and opens a closet. He pulls a navy blue fleece off a metal hanger, shuts the door, and brings it to me.

"Thanks," I say as I start pulling it on over my head.

"So?" He smiles at me. I can see the multitude of colors swirling in his eyes and the candle flame reflected against the colors. It makes his eyes look like they are on fire.

"Well, first I need to take your hand," I say. He holds his hand out but I don't pull it into my grasp just yet. "Don't freak out though, okay?"

He furrows his eyebrows. "Is it going to hurt?"

"No, but don't freak out if my eyes look crazy," I warn him.

He momentarily drops his hand since I've still yet to grasp it. "Like?" he asks, prodding me to explain more.

"They turn white. And, well, I won't be able to see," I answer.

He gives a nervous laugh and shakes his head. "I guess that's all I'm getting out of you. It's a good thing I trust you with my life."

I smile big. "Yes, and your heart. This won't be dangerous, just relax." I hold my hand out for him.

He doesn't hesitate putting his hand in mine.

I gasp when the world goes black. I can faintly hear Tony gasp too. Then the memories start flooding in.

I see Tony as a young boy. He's sitting at the table in the cabin, anxiously waiting for his parents. The lights dim in the dining room. Then his mom and dad come walking in, holding a cake topped with five lit candles.

His mom sings happy birthday in the most beautiful voice. His dad adds, "And many more," at the end of the song. They place the chocolate cake in front of him. It's his favorite flavor.

Tony's little brown eyes are lit with excitement as he closes them and blows out the candles. I hear his wish as if he said it aloud. He wishes for a bright red fire engine truck. My heart warms as I think of such an innocent request. He opens his eyes, and there sitting in front of him is a large present wrapped in red paper that's decorated with Dalmatians in fire hats. He lets out a squeal as he looks from the present to his parents.

They give him a nod, letting him know that he can open it.

He grabs the paper and quickly tears it to shreds. Inside sits a brand new, red fire truck equipped with buttons that make siren sounds, ladders that pull out, and a small fire hose that reaches down to a fake fire hydrant. He thinks that this is the best birthday he's ever had.

....

We fast-forward a few years. Tony looks to be about ten years old. He's sitting on the couch with his mom, who is reading him Alice in Wonderland. Dinner is on the table but they haven't touched it yet. Tony's stomach growls, but he knows that they need to wait for his father to return.

The lock on the front door jiggles. It opens and in comes his father. Young Tony feels scared when he sees his dad's tear-stained face.

His mom jumps up from the couch and runs to her husband. "Oh no," she says sadly as she throws her hands around her husband.

"He was so young. Tony's age." His dad cries into his

mom's shoulder.

She hugs him tighter. "I know, honey, I know." With the last word, she loses it too and both of them drop to their knees crying.

Tony feels confused, scared, and sad. His eyes tear up as he walks cautiously over to his parents. He sits down next to them and they pull him into their embrace.

"We love you so much, Tony," his dad tells him. His dad sits back on his heels and wipes the tears from his face. He looks into Tony's little eyes. "We lost your cousin Joshua today."

Tony's heart drops. Joshua was his best friend. Because of the virus, they rarely get to see each other except for during the holidays. Tony tries to tell himself that his dad means that Joshua got lost, like the time he got separated from his mom at the grocery store and couldn't find her for several minutes. In his heart, he knows that he's fooling himself. Joshua is dead, just like his grandparents are dead, just like his teacher died last year, just like the nice old lady next door who always made him chocolate chip cookies died. They are gone. Tony wonders when his time will come.

....

I'm whooshed into another memory. This time Tony looks to be the same age he is now. I notice the shelter in the background. Tony watches his parents as they freak out about what they are going to do. They aren't going into the shelter and it's so hot outside. The officials shoo them away from the area. They walk along with throngs of other rejects, towards the forest.

Tony sees his dad speaking to an old, grumpy man

in a white tank top and boxer shorts, Lee. He overhears Lee complain about the government as they begin talking about a plan to set up a safe house.

Tony joins in on the conversation and offers to be of assistance in any way he can. His dad looks at him with pride. His mom looks at him with scared eyes. She only wants her family to be safe. That's all she ever wanted. But Tony wants to be a man. He wants to step up and help in any way he can. These people will need him to be strong.

They walk for a ways in the stifling heat. At least a hundred people have joined together. As they walk, more and more run after them. Nobody wants to be left alone.

They find a Holiday Inn. A strong man finds a crowbar in an abandoned car and jimmies the door open. They start filing into the hot hotel.

Everyone finds their rooms. His parents pick one on the first floor. "Heat rises," his dad said, when they opened the door.

Tony's mom sits on the bed looking scared. She pulls out the small black box that the official gave her. "We need to take the yellow shot," she says quietly. Her hands are shaking.

His dad sits next to his wife on the bed. He puts his arm around her. "We will all be okay, babe," he tells her.

His mom tries to smile but she can't.

Tony sits on the bed adjacent from his parents. "Don't worry, Mom. Dad and I will take care of you."

His mom looks up at him with love. He knows that she is seeing the ten-year-old that she used to read to every night, instead of the nineteen-year-old man that he's become.

He doesn't mind though. He knows that his parents love him and that's all that matters.

Tony pulls out his black box from his pocket. Without thinking about it, he grabs the yellow shot and injects himself with it. His parents seem stunned at first, but they quickly follow suit.

. . . .

Tony sits in a room by himself. Things have been changing around the hotel. People have been dying. Several people's eyes have turned red. They've injected themself with the red shot. He shivers as he thinks of his parents newly red eyes. They want him to take the shot but he doesn't want to.

The door busts open and Tony looks up. His dad is standing in the doorway, looking angry. "I told you to take the shot, son." His mom comes up behind her husband and stares at her son with her red eyes.

"And I told you that I won't take it. I'm your son, but I'm also an adult and I've made my decision," he says.

"He has to take it," Tony's mom says to her husband.

His dad nods his head and starts advancing. Tony jumps from his bed and darts across the bed, faster than lightning. He sees the red shot in his mom's hand.

"This is for the best, Tony. We can all be together," she tells him.

His stomach rolls with nausea as he thinks about the changes he's seen in his parents. The quick flashes of anger, the loss of emotion, and the disconnect they seem to have from humanity.

Tony's dad backs him into a corner. Tony knows he's

going to have to fight. He doesn't anticipate his father punching him first. Tony's head jerks back at the impact. Stars cross his eyes. His dad tackles him to the ground as his mom grabs the needle.

"Stop!" a woman's voice calls from the other side of the bed. I can't see her.

His mom hesitates and then lifts her lip in a snarl. Tony struggles under his dad's grip. "No!" he yells to his mom when she turns back to him and stabs him in the arm with the needle. Before she gets a chance to inject the fluid into his bloodstream, a gunshot rings out.

The sound is deafening. His face crumples as his mom falls slowly to the ground by his side.

"Noooooo!" his father roars. He jumps up and turns towards whoever just shot his wife. "I'll kill you!" His voice and his face are contorted with rage. He runs forward, fists raised, and another gunshot sounds off in the room.

Tony looks down at the needle that is still sticking out of his arm. He pulls it out with a shaking hand.

The woman comes over to where he can see her. She places the gun on the bed. Her eyes are sad and horror-stricken. "I'm so sorry. They wouldn't stop," she whispers.

Tony can't say anything. He just blinks. But I know this woman that killed Tony's parents to save his life. Her name is Alice. She is my mother.

. . . .

I'm back in the clearing, the day I came out of the shelter. I can see myself through Tony's eyes. I'm hovering over my mom, trying to heal her. He knows he shouldn't let me be

near her, but he instinctively trusts me against his own better
judgment.

When he sees my mom wake up and me falling limp
next to her, a fierce, protective quality reverberates within him.
He runs to my side and pulls me into his arms. I'm passed out
from exhaustion. He carries me back to the safe house.

....

I see Tony teaching me to throw a knife. He notices
how nice my hair smells and wishes that he could get to know
me better. The memory of me in the vision whirls around on
him and accuses him of trying to hit on me.

He can't help but think how beautiful I am when I'm
angry.

....

I'm caught up in our first kiss on the canoe. I feel it as
if I were inside Tony. His feelings of love for me fill every part
of his mind and heart until the world goes red.

....

I see him looking for me in the woods. The red and
orange leaves are floating down like snowflakes that fall to
the earth. He wants to find me, to see me, to kiss me, but he
also doesn't want to go near me because he knows that he's
dangerous. Zack hasn't taken him over for days, but he has no
idea how long it will last. He can only hope that he's broken
free of his grasp.

He sees me in the trees and his heart flutters with hope.

....

I'm pulled to earlier today. When he told me that he
loved me. He means every word of it. I make him feel whole. I

am his family now. He will do anything for me. He loves me.

....

I open my eyes. At first, I can see nothing. My senses are heightened. The world is dark, but I can hear Tony's heavy breathing. I can feel his warm hand in mine. I can smell the mixture of soap and earth. Then slowly, my vision comes back. I see a blurry Tony in front of me and then my eyes focus.

His eyes are solid white, the only contrast are the pupils and the small dot of red. I try to look away because it's so bizarre and strange. Then I see the colors flood back into his irises. He blinks a few times and then focuses his eyes on me.

He opens his mouth to say something but no words come out. I know in that instant that he has seen my memories just as I've seen his.

He pulls me to him and crushes his lips to mine. The kiss is as intense as it is filled with pure, unadulterated love. We hold on tightly, having a new understanding of the love we each feel for one another. To truly know how someone really feels, it's indescribable. To know or to have experienced the most important events in their lives with them, it forms an unbreakable bond. It's the biggest boost of confidence, of strength, of heart-feeling, warm goodness.

I know now that no matter what our future brings, we'll be okay. Even if we are hunted forever, torn apart, murdered, sold for blood, whatever it may be, I know that I have lived my life. Love like this doesn't come around often, and for me to find it at such a young age is a blessing. For this, I am truly grateful.

"I love you," Tony says as he leans his forehead against mine.

"I love you too," I whisper.

...To Be Continued

Eye colors and the abilities they correlate to:

**Dark Green**- Ability to read minds and hear thoughts. (Willow's first gift. Willow's original eye color: brown. Willow also absorbs other people's gifts when she is around them for a certain period of time. They still don't know how this is possible but some believe it's because she has a bit of Reaper in her. However, there is one major difference between Willow and a Reaper: Willow is still in touch with her humanity.)

**Dark Blue**- Ability to heal. (Alec's gift. Alec's original eye color: Emerald Green)

**Hazel-yellow/green**- Ability to compel people and make them do or believe what you tell them. (Zack's gift. Zack's original eye color: light brown)

**Purple**- Ability to turn invisible (Claire's gift. Claire's original eye color: icy blue)

**Brown**- Ability to change molecular structure and walk or pass through objects. (Connor's gift. Connor's original eye color- black)

**Light Blue**- Ability to see through people's abilities

or see when someone is using a gift. (Candy's gift. Candy's original eye color: light brown)

Neon Yellow- Ability to possess great strength, speed, agility and immunity. Rarely, if ever, does someone with this ability get sick. (Willow's mom, whose name is Alice, Sebastian and Tony's gift. As well as everyone else in the first compound. Alice and Sebastian's original eye color: Baby Blue. Tony's original eye color: Hazel Green.

Copper Orange- Ability to see visions of the near future. This is an ability that is new to everyone. Nobody knows how far in the future this ability will allow it's possessor to see, but currently Willow's dad has only been able to see a few minutes and no more than an hour ahead of time. In addition, with the knowledge of what lies ahead, they have been able to change the future outcome. For example, Willow didn't die during the attack on the hotel like the dad foresaw. (Willow's dad: Henry's gift.)

Black- Ability to read other people's emotions and intentions. In addition this ability allows the possessor to control the emotions of others. (Erik's gift.)

Red- Reapers, steal other people's abilities and drain their life from them. Not a lot is known about this power. Some believe that once a Reaper takes from someone that they only possess the ability for a limited period of time. This requires them to continually search for abilities to consume or in other words to help them power up. Because the process of reaping takes a lot of energy and a few minutes to completely drain a person, they don't bother using their powers on the people with yellow eyes.

After all, the Reapers currently possess this ability since it was their first gift before they took the red shot that was supposed to cause instant death. Instead that shot caused the death of their humanity.

Gold- Telekinesis. Ability to move objects with one's mind. (Marya and John's gift.)

Grey/Silver- A gift we know little about. All we know is that the one person Willow has met with this eye color was not susceptible to Willow's other powers. In fact, she had to truly trust the person in order to allow a gift to work. (Jennifer's gift.)

White- Allows the person with the gift to see the entire life story of the other person with a single touch. It also causes them to go blind. In Morgan's case, he had his wife, Audrey help him see. (Morgan's gift, Erik's brother)

CONNECT WITH US

We would love to hear from you! Please come visit us:

Facebook:
http://www.facebook.com/eleseries

Twitter:
Courtney: http://www.twitter.com/nuckelsc
Rebecca: http://www.twitter.com/midnitebeckie

Webpage:
http://www.eleseries.com

ABOUT THE AUTHORS

Rebecca and Courtney are downhome country girls powered by chocolate and other random late night cravings. Coined in southern twang they bring new meaning to the word y'all. BFI's since the 6th grade, with a knack for getting into sticky situations, has resulted in countless ideas to write about for years to come.

ACKNOWLEDGEMENTS

Wow, God has blessed us to be able to do something that before had only been a pipe dream. We had no idea when we started on this adventure that we would finish one book, let alone four books. We are extremely grateful for the success he has granted us and for his biggest blessing of all, our Lord Jesus. *(Philippians 4:13)*

We appreciate all of the support we have received from book blogs, our favorite Facebook pages, our family and friends and most of all from our fans. Your encouragement kept us writing. All of your Facebook posts, Goodreads comments and emails that told us that you loved our books, made our hearts soar and made us want to write even better for you. Thank you to everyone who has taken the time to review our book and thank you to everyone who continues to read our work. A shout out to Cynthia Shepp for doing wonders for our story. You really do have a way with words!

To Marya Heiman with Strong Image Editing: Have we told you how much we love you today?!? Words cannot express our gratitude for all you do. We just can't thank you enough. Where would we be without you?

Last but not least: a giant thank you to our Awesome Sauce Street Team who are out there on the front lines helping us spread the word about our books. We love you all! Carly Bel-air, Claire Taylor, Lauren Harrington, Brenna Harden, Jamie Cross, Ashley Wiggins, Ashley Wood, Mia Melone, Veronica Morfi, Laura Martinez, Angela Stone, Terri Dion, Kim Culbertson, Shona Lawrence, Lauren Dootson, Dyan Brown, Cynthia Shepp, Kendall McCubbin, Lela Lawing, Kathleen Guardado, Tonya Bunch, Lisa Sasso, Natlie Idrogo, Heather Alexander, Brittany Willis, Marya Heiman, Melanie Newton, Alicia Hall, Amy Stogner, Colleen Reilly, Jovhanna Caltzontzi, Kristy Hamilton, Rebekah Ashworth, Heather Piantanida-pipes, Michele Skinner, Cassie Hoffman, Kristin Kim, Nikki Archer, Irayda Quezada, Karissa Stephens, Jamie Miller, Krystal Marlein, Pam Mandigo, Melanie Martin, Lori Fenn, Mayra Arellano, Cassie Chavez, Samantha Trusdale and Jamie Cross. These names are in no particular order. You are all amazing and we are so grateful to have you!

CPSIA information can be obtained
at www.ICGtesting.com
Printed in the USA
LVOW10s0505290917
550515LV00001B/25/P